THE WITCHES OF SAN PEDRO DEL INGLESI

THOMAS WALTERS

Inquiries and Book Orders should be addressed to:

Great Writers Media
Email: info@greatwritersmedia.com
Phone: (302) 918-5570
16192 Coastal Highway, Lewes DE 19958, USA

ISBN: 978-1-954908-71-0 (sc)
ISBN: 978-1-954908-72-7 (ebk)

Rev 05/18/2021

CONTENTS

BRENDA'S LAST
FLING BUT TWO

BRENDA HAD BEEN WIDOWED SOME months and she was still feeling pretty low. So she thought about buying a nice little 'pad' for herself in Spain, on the Costa Del Sol. But Jim had always been a bit mean with the money so she didn't mind spending a good wack of his estate on a luxurious villa in a little enclave of similar ex pat accommodations called San Pedro Del Inglesi in the hills above Marbella. She hadn't been there more than a few days when she felt lonely -most of the residents had decamped to England for the Summer leaving only a few renting relatives whose constant noise round the pool twenty four hours a day left her bereft and bemused. So one warm evening she drove out along the coastal road and came to Manuel's Bar. She felt a bit left out at first as there only seemed to be men there. No women. The men had their jackets around their shoulders and pointed their cigarettes in the air rather a lot and everytime she tried to smile at them they gave her quick up-and-down looks and blew smoke into her face. She got quite depressed and wondered at first whether it was her personal freshness -it was a very warm night-but her numerous unguents had been well-used that evening and she knew it couldn't be that. She couldn't understand it. She had always taken great care over her appearance and was very good for fifty nine (well 61¼ to be precise) and looked more like forty nine. Her figure was hardly svelte or even plump but it certainly wasn't gross. There may have been a few wrinkles on the surface and a bit of cellulite here and there but underneath it all there beat the lusty heart of a forty- odd year old.

Suddenly she looked across the smoke-filled room and saw a balding, fat middle-aged Englishman propped up against the bar staring into space with glassy eyes, he looked lost. She thought, "Ugh! Who'd want that!" But then something happened that intrigued her. He quickly picked up his empty coffee cup, held it high for a moment, looked into it as though it were transparent and then deftly stuck his tongue into it. That tongue darted here there and everywhere and in a trice he had thoroughly explored every portion of it. Finally after one spectacular lunge he had retrieved that very last grain of sugar that had been clinging so tenaciously to the bottom of the cup. Brenda marvelled at this in a weary, time-worn sort of way.

"He may not be much to look at! He's a slob, let's face it, but I bet he knows how to make a girl feel young again."

She sauntered over to him. After a while he noticed that she was there and at that instant stopped standing on her foot.

He said: "Hello gorgeous! Would you like to join me in a coffee?"

"You're the only one here who's asking. Yes I would!" she replied eagerly.

After she had paid for the cup of coffee, he neatly drained it to the last drop and promptly put it down on the saucer. He then asked, head swaying, if she wanted another. She smiled and replied: "No dear, but could you do something for me please?"

"Anything you like sweetheart! What did you have in mind?"

She mimed with the cup, "Could you lick.You know?"

"What here darling? In front of all these people?"

"Get off me! Not me you clown, the cup -like you did just a moment ago?"

"Oh! I thought you meant."

"I know what you thought Einstein! And it strikes me you'd be the only one here who'd know how to do it but just do the business with the cup.

From that magic moment their relationship blossomed. They began to see a great deal more of each other until Bill finally popped the question. He had not long buried his 'spouse' but he didn't think there was very much point in dawdling at their age and Brenda gratefully concurred.

They decided to sell his Villa and live in hers at San Pedro Del Inglesi and they lived happily there ever after until he dropped dead one day after straining to clean out a larger than usual coffee mug, leaving Brenda to pick up the pieces and mop up the sugar. She paused for a moment and a tear came to her eye. She remembered that magic moment in Manuel's Bar.

Definitely Brenda's
Last Fling But One

Undaunted she collected the insurance money and planned another get-away holiday.

"Here I go again!" she mused.

But then she looked at herself yet again in the new gilt-framed mirror she had recently purchased in one of her early morning ritual forays into the labyrinthine heart of Marbella's old town -Coffee, Orange Square-Purchase -Villa for lunch-Siesta What she saw was herself looking into a mirror at herself looking into a mirror at herself.......

"This time! Maybe this time!." she trilled. "Not quite Lisa Minnelli in 'Cabaret'," she mused, "but the same bloody sentiments."

'Cruises for the Over Forties!' seemed about right. She didn't want to take any more risks with the over fifties. She had buried two husbands and to bury a third might seem like over-zealous planning. She was nothing if not a stickler for details in her men, in her money and indeed in all matters to do with her life. That's why she had survived. That's why she had seen off two husbands and buried two more. That's why she kept at bay both cancers and coronaries which had taken their toll of her less careful friends. Not that she'd ever made any mistakes you understand. Her men were just not up to the very high opinion she had of them at the start. They didn't have the stamina. Men just weren't very strong. You could almost draw a graph of it. A straight line. The stronger they looked, the weaker they were. But this time…Maybe this time! (she lilted) she'd pick a winner or if not a winner she'd settle for a five year guarantee plus insurance policies.

This is how she met Trevor. Trevor was an early -retired, widowed Headmaster with no family ties who lived like a hermit at No. 15 San Pedro Del Inglesi until Brenda had winkled him out to attend the official champagne opening of her patio conversion (with coach lamps). He had a half share in an English Language school in Estepona but otherwise busied himself with pottering around his collection of cacti and orchids. He was fifty five, looked forty five and gave the impression that he could still take a few assemblies and tick off a few teachers. He liked walking, so did she. he preferred sports to books and still kept his hand in at village cricket matches when he returned to the family home in Berkshire (his mother's) every summer and he never missed a test match. He was a practical no-nonsense man just as she was a practical no-nonsense woman. She was glad he wasn't intellectual. She distrusted intellectuals. They were nearly always fidgeting, dithering, indecisive people who would almost certainly succumb to the first real problem they had to face. Her mathematical cast of mind imagined a graph with 90% of cancer/coronary patients being intellectual worriers (in red) with only 10% being hearty, no-nonsense, outdoor extroverts (in blue). Although it did cross her mind that Trevor might conceivably be one of the 'blue' ones -none the less dead for being blue. However, she dismissed the thought instantly (as she dismissed most of her thoughts) as being the senile ramblings of an old fart who ought to know better. Thought was the privilege of the young who had the time and opportunity to indulge it. She couldn't afford to think. Sixty one (61¼ to be precise) was a time for getting on with it before it was too late. They had two contented years together and then one day they had motored up to Ronda for lunch at a favourite haunt when...

"A penny for your thoughts Brenda?" Trevor quizzed eagerly.

"You'll have to do a good deal better than that dear if you want to gain access to my mind!" She cackled.

"Would a hundred pesetas cover it?"

"Just buy me a drink and shut up!"

He was a long time coming back from the bar until it suddenly dawned on her that the corpse the crowds were bending over was Trevor........

Letter From
A Retired
Headmaster

Dear All,

I expect you're all agog, wondering what's become of me. Just to set your minds at rest I thought I'd put pen to paper and let you into my thoughts.

It's wonderful being retired. You can get up whenever you like. You know how I used to be a stickler for getting to school on time in the mornings? Well, I don't care anymore and it's nice.

Brenda has turned out to be a real pal. She always greets me with a nice smile when I bring her breakfast up every morning, and by the time I've got back from the Hypermercado with her newspapers and magazines, she's singing in the shower and filling the house with her version of 'Madame Butterfly'. The housework doesn't take me very long and by the time I've washed up it's time to take her into Marbella.

We usually have a nice lunch in the Plaza Naranjos and Brenda always has a good giggle when I tell her I've left my wallet in the villa. It's getting to be quite a habit this and we nearly always have a good laugh about it.

After Siesta time I spend most of the rest of the afternoons doing a bit of gardening or doing odd jobs about the house. Brenda always finds something for me to do, she likes to keep me busy. Evening soon comes round and on those evenings we don't dine out (very few!) I like to do the cooking. By the time I've finished the washing up and ironed my things for the following day (I don't trust Brenda with the iron or the lawnmower) -I'm ready for an early bed.

Sometimes Brenda wakes me up in the middle of the night with a persistent tap on my shoulder.

"What's the matter my pet?" say I.

"Oh nothing much!" replies she and then turns over.

I put it down to worry about the villa. We've had so many break-ins in our part of Marbella recently and one Englishwoman was raped in her own bedroom.

"Not me!" says Brenda wistfully, she will have her little joke about it.

Women! Always wanting something. Now she's even talking about separate holidays.

I must confess sometimes I have a yearning to be back at school taking assemblies or helping children with their basketry or even going over stock lists with Mr Johns. By the way, if you ever see Mr Johns,

tell him I'm interested in buying a couple of paint-
ings of his, the ones he once showed me with the
ornate gold frames -he'll know the ones I mean. I
thought those frames were really beautiful. Mind you
if his asking price goes above £50 tell him to forget it.
It's just that those frames would go nicely on two wall
spaces at the back of our kitchen on either side of my
wife's magic mirror ('mirror! Mirror! on the wall?')
Brenda reckons that every time she sees me in it I get
richer. She's been watching me a lot recently -I'd better check those stocks and shares! Pass on my regards
to all, especially Mrs Bernstein. Tell Pete he can rely
on my references for years to come and also tell Alice
Gunns that I miss her and I'm having the time of my
life (she'll know what I mean and so will he).

I wish you all the best of British luck with your
new head. Yours Trevor Barratt.

HOSPITAL HERE
I COME!!

GOING THROUGH A DEAD ONE'S things is never a
pleasant task but Brenda had had plenty of practice.
Yet she was quite shocked to see the letter Trevor had
written, but never posted, to his erstwhile colleagues
at his school in Berkshire. It seemed to show a disre-
spect towards her and a certain levity that she didn't
know he had possessed. Must be careful next time,
she thought, as she burned his things.

It was summer once again and life was becoming
boring again at San Pedro until a routine examina-
tion at her local private clinic had revealed something
that needed looking into. Dr Joselito Juan, the exciting young surgeon to whom she had been referred,
jokingly asided that it could well be a blur on the
X-Ray but he didn't want to take any chances. He
had pawed and pummeled her around a lot, knead-
ing the hills and valleys of her tummy, until she was
quite prepared for anything he had on offer in the
way of specialist treatment. But nevertheless she was
somewhat relieved when he suggested:

"I honestly don't think it's anything but we'd better do an exploratory to be sure…un poco..un poco operation…for a youthful senora!" He beamed as he buttoned her blouse

It would mean a spell in hospital. She was quite excited at the thought of the break in the dull round. The surgery was booked for the following October. She would throw a party at San Pedro Del Inglesi just before she went in -It would coincide with the return of the residents from Britain and would give them all a chance to renew their appreciation of her. She cackled at her own outrageousness.

The party turned out to be a great success -"I must go into hospital more often" she mused, in front of Trevor's favourite mirror. At least she thought she had dissipated all those hole-in-the-corner, ugly rumours about her marriages which she dismissed to everyone's obvious amusement as 'monogamous mistakes'.

As she packed her things away neatly the night before her admission her mind raced ahead excitedly to the thought of being prodded and poked and thoroughly examined by some well-mannered but decidedly Spanish consultant. Dr Ravi, however, didn't quite live up to her expectations. He was short, fat, bald and spoke little English. She didn't mind a certain amount of hair on her men as long as it was evenly distributed in all the right places. He seemed to be devoid of hair everywhere except in his nostrils. "Do you feel any pain Mrs Barratt??" He had asked her twice. Her symptoms hadn't caused her any pain but Dr Ravi's appearance had caused her a great deal of displeasure. She chuckled inwardly at the thought of this going on her record card.

"Mrs Barratt are you listening to what I'm saying?"

"Oh I'm sorry doctor. I was daydreaming for a moment. No I don't feel any pain. I feel fine!" she replied.

"There doesn't appear to be anything wrong with you so we're sending you home tomorrow."

Brenda didn't know what to feel. She was naturally glad that there was nothing seriously wrong with her. On the other hand she missed the prospect of an exciting operation with a long lazy convalescence with medical 'flunkeys' buzzing around attending to her every need. You could hardly call three days - 'major surgery' -What would her commiserating friends make of all this? They might start rumour-mongering again. Oh dear.

It was as she made her way down the steps outside the hospital entrance that she suddenly slipped and broke her hip. The agony of the experience was a check to her constant reveries about the drama and romance of hospitalisation. As they wheeled her slowly into Orthopaedic Ward 9, her heart sank as she glanced at the serried ranks of geriatrics lying open-mouthed like goldfish, staring at the ceiling. The depression momentarily displaced the excruciating pain. But then as she was laid to rest on the bed she heard the all-too-familiar tones:

Welcome back Mrs Barratt!" said Dr Ravi smiling roguishly. The excruciating pain came flooding back to her.

DEATHS TO FORGET-
MARRIAGES TO
REMEMBER!

THE CONVALESCENCE TOOK LONGER THAN she thought nevertheless she was soon back at San Pedro and her myriad friends and neighbours were once more dancing attendance on her. But no sooner was she up on her feet than she heard of the death of her Uncle Bernard from Norfolk. The awful thing about getting older was that funerals became more frequent and closer to home When one met old friends one was pleasantly surprised that they were still there. Brenda was getting pretty fed-up of the number of her friends that would not stay alive. It was a constant and unpleasant reminder to her that she was moving slowly but inexorably up the queue outside St Peter's Gate.

Uncle Bernard was 94 and the family Nobel Prize winner for old age. It was a comfort to all surviving Barratts that Bernard had lived to such a great age because it meant that genetically it was at least possible that others in the family might also live that long - but preferably without the double incontinence and blindness. Uncle Bernard's condition gradually improved for several months until he finally died during a particularly beautiful week in May. The funeral was one of those ad hoc humanist affairs, terribly pretentious and acutely embarrassing with all sorts of odd people getting up and reading bad poems or telling hopelessly irrelevant anecdotes about the departed. Reading between the lines one could tell a few old scores had been settled. Bernard had made as many enemies as he had friends but all was forgiven at the reading of the will when it was revealed that the old boy had left his £350,000 estate to a dogs' home. The prevailing sentiment being, as one long-lost sister put it, 'At least the others aren't getting anything either!'

On the way back in the plane Brenda reflected on the awfulness of it all. At least at the funerals of one's nearest and dearest one had grief to preoccupy oneself with. But at the funerals of more distant relatives after the first few token tears one could only be painfully objective about the true horror of this spectacle of human frailty. She vowed that she'd never attend another funeral as long as she lived.

She got back to the villa in June. It was creepily quiet as the residents had gone and the tourists hadn't arrived yet. Even Ahmed had long gone after mowing the lawns and turning on the sprinklers. Nobody at all, nothing at all, only the pattering of the waters from the sprinklers.

She sat down in the hallway with her bags and just cried. It was very unlike her. She was quite angry with herself for doing it. But it was purely involuntary and was, she persuaded herself, the result of accumulated griefs spanning the previous five years and more. First Jim, then Bill, and as if fate was determined to go in threes -Trevor. By about seven in the evening she was all cried out and looking in her favourite mirror she even started to giggle a little -hysteria no doubt- as she watched the mascara coursing like dark streams down the ravaged hills of her cheekbones. Her giggles turned to cackles and then to raucous laughter.

"You silly old cow! You look like a witch. You are a bloody witch! The witch of San Pedro Del Inglesi!" Her hands simulated horns and she made a mock charge at the mirror.

"You're also a little tipsy Brenda Barratt of Basingstoke". She giggled again and poured herself a large G & T. and toasted herself at the mirror.

"To you Brenda Barratt, aged sixty-ish, and why shouldn't you laugh a little too?"

She reflected that the comedies of her life were just as worthy of attention as her tragedies. Her two chief comedies were of course her two divorces -the ones she'd 'seen off' as she put it. There was the terribly good-looking Adrian to whom she was passionately hitched at the ridiculously young age of seventeen. The marriage lasted precisely nine months. Her self-righteous father, whose whole life revolved around a string of carpet shops in North London, had strongly disapproved of the liaison right from the outset and they had had to elope. Her mother had died in childbirth -and she had been brought up by a series of au pairs, nannies, maids etc. She was the only child and her father by turns worshipped her and terrorised her if she stepped out of line. He tried to put her in the place of the wife he had lost but ended up losing her as well.

"To see the look on your face Daddy when you knew the game was up," she cackled," it was worth it!"

After nine months Adrian upped and ran off with a plumber's mate with whom he had been secretly having it off for at least six of those nine months. Adrian had been old enough to be Brenda's father (he was forty two) but ended up behaving more like her mother. He owned a string of hairdressing salons and had branched out into saunas and massage parlours. He had apparently met 'Steve' when he was repairing a newly-installed shower in one of his West End luxury saunas. It was 'love at first shower', Steve had remarked at their final showdown. Brenda felt nothing except humorous relief. After all, it was through Steve that she had gained her freedom from her father. She never spoke to her father again but when he died he left her everything.

Then there was Marcus who was more her own age. He was an engineer who had engineered his way to the West Indies somewhere and had never been seen since. That was thirty odd years ago. Marcus was an odd ball, not quite in the same way as Adrian, but equally funny in retrospect. He was one of those dithering intellectuals she had grown to distrust. He was very good-natured but totally absent-minded. One day he'd gone off to work as usual and had never returned. His firm had said that he was working for various sugar companies in Trinidad and British Guiana (as it was then, Guyana now). They seemed a little surprised that she wasn't with him. She had been left with two boys to bring up on her own. Fortunately Marcus's 'hoity toity' elder brother Lord Alfred De Penchester had stepped in to take care of the boys' future but there had been a price to pay for this. The phone rang urgently to wake her from her reverie. It was her niece Sarah from Tonbridge, Lord Alfred's daughter, who announced tearfully the sad demise of Great Aunt Mildred, Brenda's Aunt on Marcus's side. Brenda expressed her commiserations and put the phone down. She relaxed and poured herself another G & T. She felt quite detached from Aunt Mildred and indeed any other person who might care to die on her in the immediate future (she giggled). So Aunt Mildred was dead indeed. Now that was a death to forget.

A Cornucopia
of Religions

She was determined that Trevor would be her
last foray into the matrimonial stakes. But the more
decided she became about this the more depressed
she became. She couldn't really understand it because
she thought that by now she had become inured to
it all. It was not as though she was short of a bob or
two. The wreckage of her domestic life did contain
the buried treasure of insurance money and she was
really quite comfortable with the regular income that
an accumulation of pensions, endowments, matured
policies etc was providing for her. She had never
been a spendthrift and could now reap the reward of
a lifetime of abstemiousness. But that was just it. She
didn't know what to do with it all. Habits of a lifetime can't be broken that easily. She felt bored, guilty,
depressed and vulnerable to the likes of Lester Omar
Pearson Junior of Cornucopia Unlimited.

Brenda was giving herself one of her 'treats', as
she called them, a five star weekend at an exclusive
hotel near Porto Banus. She was sitting in the Sunset
Bar having her usual preprandials when up bounced

Omar, a tanned and energetic fifty year old, with an expensive but slightly out-of-kilter toupee. She felt sorry for him, which was her first mistake. He hailed from Atlantic City and claimed to be in Malaga for an international conference of theologians.

"Why would theologians want to come to Malaga? Anyway you don't look like a theologian to me. I thought they wore dog collars and were thin, weedy men in gold-rimmed spectacles? You look too healthy to be a theologian!"

"Kind of you to say so ma'am. But I have a Doctorate in Systematic Theology and Philosophy from the University of Connecticut. I'm a lay theologian so I don't wear a clerical collar."

He then proceeded to tell her of the benefits to humanity that he hoped to bring through 'Cornucopia Unlimited'. It all sounded terribly dubious to Brenda but she threw her somewhat better judgment to the winds temporarily because she was lonely and this man was entertaining her whatever his ulterior motives were -and they were becoming more obvious by the minute. Apparently his business was providing a consultancy service in World Religions and 'value systems'. He argued quite convincingly that people were bemused and confused by the plethora of different religions and they didn't know which way to turn for faith. This is where Omar came in. He said he was an expert and he was well qualified to lead people through, what he called, 'a spiritual minefield'.

"So where's the catch?" enquired Brenda still holding on to her sobriety in spite of four G & Ts with ice and lemon.

"There is no catch -except in the spiritual sense! Of course I have to charge a fee. I have a living to earn and I can't do this sort of thing for nothing."

"How much do you charge?" she replied, anxious to get to the point before the gin and tonics got to her. She felt vaguely embarrassed at her own question because her subconscious had clearly seen the implications of it before she had.

"Five hundred guineas, the price of an ordinary television set. Surely the salvation of one's immortal soul was worth the price of a T.V.!!?"

Brenda was by now doubled up with laughter and it took two more G & Ts to calm her down.

"I don't want to save my soul love but I'd be happy to take out a lease on my body!" she screamed in between her hysterics. By now the other occupants of this small cocktail bar were all looking on disapprovingly, two prim young couples walked out - the elderly ones seemed content to watch. Brenda didn't give them the satisfaction.

"O.K. big boy! Five hundred guineas is a deal Come on! Let's see what you're made of!"

With a Mae West flourish she left the bar with Lester Omar Pearson Junior trailing behind her. Never before had Brenda ever made such a spectacle of herself but it didn't all turn out quite as she had anticipated. What she wanted was to be taken for a ride, shamefully used and abused, stimulated and left high and dry. In short, she wanted her confidence boosting. What she actually got was a five weeks course on religion. She ploughed her way hopelessly through Buddhism, Shintoism, Taoism, Islam and Hinduism, but the only enlightenment that came out of it was the dawning that Omar was exactly what he said he was -no more no less. When he could see how utterly indifferent she was to the claims of any religion, he kindly returned her five hundred guineas to her and wished her well. She wasn't even left with a frisson from being fleeced. He was a perfect gentleman and she felt like a harlot that hadn't quite come up to scratch.

All her life, people, including her father and several husbands, had been warning her about being taken advantage of - usually the people who were taking the advantage. Now when she wanted someone to take advantage of her everyone was honest all of a sudden. The following Saturday there was a buzz at the door. She opened up to find a young English clergyman with a bible in his hand. It turned out that he was a sort of missionary evangelical from the local Anglican community hellbent on rescuing any stray ex-patriot sheep who might be drifting Romewards or even worse, drifting into Mediterranean hedonism (Brenda's brand of religion).

"Do you have a few moments to spare?" he said in kindly, impeccable English.

"Yes I do," she replied equally warmheartedly. "Do come in out of the heat."

An hour and a half and two carafes of Sangria later, he left without any satisfaction. No she didn't want to attend bible classes for the over sixties. No, she didn't feel any need to let Jesus into her life. No, she didn't want to join a club run by 'young Christian people'.

But yes, she did want someone to make her laugh. He couldn't oblige.

Betty Ackroyd
- A Simple Case
Of Human
Self-Sufficiency

BRENDA COULD LIVE WITHOUT A man certainly. Wasn't her own life a living proof of this? The trail of male debris stretched back over a period of nearly fifty years and she had survived them all if not virgo intacta, certainly intacta. She had all her marbles, even if the bag containing them was a little frayed at the edges.

But if she could now live without men, she couldn't live without a friend in whom she could confide and this had to be a woman. Betty Ackroyd was that friend. She was exactly the same age as Brenda almost to the day. It would seem that they had decayed at approximately the same rate so there was never any of that 'wrinkle rivalry' that had bitched up so many relationships among her female acquaintances back at San Pedro Del Inglesi. They had exactly the same pedigree in husbands, five apiece, although Betty had buried one more spouse than her friend -apparently something of a course record in her locality of Fuengirola. Even their respective bank balances tallied to the last nought. However, this last fact could only be guessed at by Brenda as some secrets are too intimate to be disclosed even between bosom pals. Yes, she knew all the details of the sexual quirks of Betty's partners but she could only estimate the extent of the inheritance yielded up at their respective deaths.

She first met Betty at an 'Over Fifties' night at a Palais de Dance, in Fuengirola- yet another place newly- opened to cater for the great mass of the elderly English who migrated there in winter to escape the ravages of their climate. It was a bit down-market for Brenda. It smelt of beer and fish and chips and looked like Southend-on-Sea, but the warm vulgarity of the place helped dispel the insularity that prolonged loneliness was beginning to instill in her.

She had ventured out that Saturday evening from her villa in San Pedro Del Inglesi with the express intention of avoiding the persistent English clergyman who had first tried to sell religion to her only two months before and had clearly not taken no for an answer. His 'Pale Galilean' spirituality was once more hovering at her door and she drove off on the pretext of 'seeing a friend' and she ended up at the 'old 'uns' club only to find to her dismay that the Rev. 'Freddy' Bartholomew had followed her there and was grinning across at her with arms akimbo. She immediately escaped on to the dance floor gyrating hopelessly to a difficult paso doble. She was rescued by Betty who, seeing her plight, ushered her to the bar in a ladies' 'excuse me' with all the dexterity and savoir faire of a seasoned campaigner in that constant and unremitting war against dance hall bores.

"Phew! That was a close one! Thanks."

She downed the proffered G & T only to spy the 'Pale Galilean' with lady friend marching towards her -their smiles flashing, their dentures matching! Betty waved her magic wand again and she was soon back on the floor 'military two-stepping' her way through the crowds to a safe haven at the tombola end. She remembered the occasion vividly. It was one of those dances that owed nothing to music and movement so much as to the desperate urge of a herd of lonely old people to hold on to each other like grim death through the winter of their social lives. As usual there were far more women than men and their floral dresses decorated the walls around the hall like the wall flowers they really were. Ah! Nights in the gardens of Spain! Ferdinand and Isabella would have turned in their graves and not to the tune of Max Bygraves either whose music droned on in the background. The few men ranged from the kinky, snappily dressed forty year olds, through the serried ranks of earnest freshly- widowed late fifty and sixty year olds, to some tired slow-foxtrotting seventy year olds and a sprinkling of cocky spry eighty year olds. Betty and Brenda danced the last waltz together by which time they had laid out the whole of their respective lives before each other and anyone else who might care to eavesdrop on their raucous conversations.

"I expect it will be the last waltz for some of them dear!" Betty commented as one puffing-billy of an old boy shunted past them with the veins standing out on his temples and a blue glistening nose with a drop, a veritable pearl, hanging precariously from the end. Brenda and Betty took to each other straight away and spent the journey back to Brenda's flat reminiscing on the different dance disasters they had adorned over the years. They seem to laugh at the same things and by the time they had arrived back at Brenda's place in San Pedro Del Inglesi they'd even got a few guffaws out of the taxi driver. This didn't unfortunately lead to a reduction in their fares but it somehow cemented their relationship -with each other that is, not the taxi driver (they were getting quite tiddly).

After a couple more G & Ts they felt they had known each other all their lives and by the early hours they had neatly laid out yet again their past histories for their mutual perusal lest they had left something important out.

"Betty you know the man you were dancing the slow-foxtrot with -the pompous-looking fellow with the bald head?"

"Yes, out with it dear, I think you're pissed!"

"No I'm not! What was I saying?"

"You were talking about 'baldy' who danced such a divine foxtrot, and you were saying it was pity he had bad breath."

"Oh yes. Well, he reminded me of a husband I had once, or once had, to be more truthful."

"Which one?"

"Do you know, I can't remember!" Brenda giggled uncontrollably.

"That makes two of us -Neither can I and I've got more to remember than you!"

"No it doesn't! We've had the same number of husbands-five!"

"So we have. It's a draw then!" Betty joined in the chorus of giggles, "and do you know. I don't miss any of them!"

Betty was a simple case of human self-sufficiency. Brenda had at last met her soul-mate.

Helping Others

Betty and Brenda now met quite regularly and planned little outings and expeditions together. The following summer they decided to venture further afield. Betty wanted to return to England in search of the haunts of her youth in South London including a goodly number of old watering holes off the Old Kent Rd. Brenda was a little apprehensive but followed in Betty's wake just for the sheer excitement of it. It was something to do. They ensconced themselves in a 'posh' hotel in Kensington but ended up finding their pleasures at the 'Horse and Trumpet' somewhere near Peckham. After one such lush evening they found their way back to their hotel a little quicker than they anticipated. The two 'business executives' they had been chit-chatting to at the bar all evening hadn't followed them down the lane as they had anticipated but had gone off in the opposite direction singing 'Men of Harlech'.

"Let's face it Betty at our age it was a little naive of us to take them at their word," said Brenda later, spooning the skin off her cafe au lait.

"You sh-peak for yourself Brenda old girl. You're pissed it -I mean you're passed it!" replied Betty whose purchase on sobriety and been loosened by her seventh gin and tonic.

"No. 'It' passed us dear -They were walking down the other side of the lane with that prissy Welsh slut from behind the bar! Bastards!"

The conversation became more and more maudlin as the early hours of the morning marched on. At three o'clock Betty was asleep but Brenda was still telling her what they were going to do the following week. They would help others. She rambled on until about four o'clock about the glories of human goodness -'the sparkling gem in the tiara of old age', as she put it. Brenda was obviously well in her cups too as in a more sober mood she was always saying how goodness was the last refuge of the desperate and the desperately old. But clearly something had been decided at subliminal level because the very next week Brenda and Betty were enrolled as 'temporary helpers' at the local 'Harmony Group for Single Parent Families' (Courtesy of Hackney Social Services).

They felt slightly out of place there because quite apart from being studiously ignored by the social worker in charge, the screaming mini-hooligans of children didn't seem to need them or anyone else for that matter but just roamed around the playground destroying everything in their wake. As for the thin chain-smoking mothers, none of them were much more than twenty five but looked forty and they were just as noisy as the kids and twice as rude.

"I don't know why you bother to come here -It's a dump! Haven't you got anything better to do.

Crikey, if I had your chances in life I'd be off on a beach somewhere!" said one pregnant rat-face, blowing smoke.

"Oh we've tried that and found it wanting!" replied Brenda, lying her way into a confrontation.

"Well, what's so bleedin' marvellous about 'ere??" The rat-face continued. There was a slight pause as the two old pals took in the obvious truth of this remark.

"Should you be smoking if you're expecting another child?" Betty questioned casually so as to change the subject. But the question wasn't as tactfully phrased as it might have been, even though it was kindly meant. The explosion came five seconds later.

"Who the bleedin' 'ell do you think you are poking your fat noses into other people's business? Why don't you fuck off and sort your own problems out. You 'do gooders' make me sick. Look! If you want to do good give me some money but you can stuff your advice right up your fannies!"

"Would £50 do?" Brenda replied calmly, grateful to have been shaken out of a mini-depression by this display of single-parent fireworks.

"Yeh, yeh! Tah! very grateful and all that. Didn't mean to shout at you like that but I sort of lost my rag when you…"

"Don't explain..Just-just take it!" interjected Brenda as she and Betty made for the door.

As they walked into the fresh air outside the vandalised community centre they felt as though they had been released from their vows. In the cocktail lounge of the Royal Grafton Hotel, Kensington, they reflected on the traumas of the day and talked about how they would spend the rest of their holiday.

"Funny how goodness brings the worst out in people!" Brenda concluded.

THE SUN RISES
IN THE WEST

BRENDA HADN'T SEEN BETTY FOR nearly two months now as she had decided to return to Spain a little earlier than either of them had anticipated. Brenda was secretly glad about this. It was nice to be able to rely on friends but you didn't want them in your pocket -or you in theirs.

It was a pleasant Saturday afternoon. It was autumn so she found herself having a stroll through Kensington Gardens and ending up buying a ticket for a concert in the Royal Albert Hall, so that took care of the evening. When you're retired and on your own there's comfort in organised time-spaces filled, time gaps plugged. The endless strivings to cheat oblivion require a 'full and active life'. She had a leisurely dinner at her hotel, the Royal Grafton, and on the wings of three gin and tonics glided into the taxi which was to whisk her to the R.A.H. This was the bit she didn't like -entering the foyer of the busy concert hall. When you're on your own, it's the worst place to be. The throngs of people greeting each other or anticipating the arrival of loved ones somehow highlight your loneliness. She made her way to her box just as the orchestra was tuning up. It was then that she noticed that she wasn't alone. A bespectacled Japanese gentleman was already ensconced in the corner. Looking up from his programme, he grinned broadly, rose and bowed respectfully.

"Sorry -my wife is already not well. I am being by myself tonight. O.K.?" said Mr Eiichiro Tagamusha in splintered-to-smithereens English.

Brenda too apologised for being a widow and on her own and expressed the hope that it wouldn't inconvenience him. It wouldn't, apparently. This insane conversation consisting of whispered apologies continued throughout the overture until 'sh-shs' from below put a stop to it. She slipped out awkwardly at the interval and returned to find that the Jap had mercifully gone. She moved her chair into a more central position in the box and had settled down to enjoy the Haydn Symphony when Mr Tagamusha returned. He had been drinking scotch and apologised noisily for his interruption. Once again there were staccato 'shushes' from the cheaper seats which inspired Brenda to apologise even more noisily for having moved her chair to the middle. Even more insistent 'shushes' joined by counter 'shushes' -a veritable symphony of shushes—stopped the noise. Brenda was thoroughly enjoying the drama of all this and was almost sorry that Haydn's music, sublime as it was, damped down the fun.

Mr Tagamusha was, as one would expect, a perfect gentleman, and offered her the one remaining stool in the bar of his hotel. This meant, unfortunately, that she was perched about eighteen inches above his head whilst he stood staring at her well-corseted navel. She felt distinctly uncomfortable, like a piece of old English porcelain about to be bought and shipped to the orient. For one brief moment she had a fantasy of herself in the jungles of the far east, tied to a tree with a sweating, semi-naked Mr Tagamusha poised to strike her to kingdom come with a shining samurai sword raised above his head.

Actually Mr Tagamusha proffered nothing more threatening than a 'Pink Lady' and her reverie was soon over. However, she reassured herself that she had gone this far with him because he was obviously a gentleman and also he seemed to have very interesting credentials. He said he was a merchant banker and was in process of negotiating financial arrangements for different Japanese companies which were over here to buy up their moribund British counterparts -whatever that meant.

At least he didn't appear to be after her money. Neverless she was still a little ambivalently concerned that he might be making a takeover bid for her body. It has to be said that she did have a sneaking little prejudice to which she had held firm over the years. However cosmopolitan her mind aspired to be, she was determined that the territory of her body, even to the utmost secret parts, should remain 'forever England'. No foreigner, even as charming as Seigo Tagamusha, would ever plant his flag in her soil, to this she was avowed. But was she a stone? She couldn't be entirely indifferent to the attentions of any man, especially one as sweet and as gentle as Seigo. Siggy was the best on offer she'd had in years and she knew she's be a bloody fool to pass it by on purely patriotic grounds. But nothing came of it.

"You bloody fool Brenda! I thought you knew better. All that wisdom, wit and experience! You behave like a simpering fourteen year old who can't remember the date of her last period!" Betty was truly scornful.

"How was I to know that the nifty Nip was on his way to Kuala Lumpur?"

"How old are you Brenda?"

"Don't remind me! Oh God Betty! I go to the bottom of the class don't I?"

"And how! Just for a moment of pleasure!"

"Pleasure? You can't accuse me of that Betty dear! He was a grandfather. He had three grownup sons with families of their own and his wife, if you please, had been to Brompton Oratory that evening and smiled at me on the stairs as I went down."

"How did you recognise her?"

"He spent half the night showing me photos. Nothing happened that's the worst of it. Nothing."

"I don't believe you!"

"He said he was tired. So was I actually! I was glad of the excuse to tell the truth."

"Oh never mind petal. Perhaps he'll see you again after Kuala Lumpur? And don't look at me with those soulful eyes or I'll think it's the Palais de Dance all over again!"

"Thank you Betty 'Wonderwoman' Ackroyd. When it's your turn to suffer I'll give you the same amount of sympathy and understanding in return!"

SUNSET AT SAN PEDRO DEL INGLESI

SHE WAS GLAD TO BE back at San Pedro Del Inglesi which was intended to be just another 'pad', a place of transit between one of life's episodes and another but it was beginning to turn into a sort of home, she was putting down roots at last. It wasn't long before Betty had sold up and was moving into No. 2, the vacant villa next door.

Through her pair of highly-prized, achromatic-lensed, binoculars Brenda could see all she needed to see now. Not the Sierra Blanca, which she had observed countless times from her bedroom patio when she came out for midnight moon bathing and midday sun bathing and although she had viewed it with a kind of proprietorial pleasure for the last few years of her retirement she didn't know what that mountain was called in Spanish or any other language. Ah! such are the English abroad. They don't feel the need to know anything about local culture. Their own self-confidence and self-sufficiency, hermetically sealed them off from any real contact. But Brenda did need to know all she needed to know.

There was that Essex family from Braintree or was it the brainless family from Essex at No. 6. -but you didn't need to use binoculars to view their antics! They were everywhere. A blond tribe of semi-clad children of indeterminate sex between the ages of four and ten, whose cries and whoops could be heard daily round the pool during the holiday periods -mercifully only during the holiday periods. Dad was a prosperous used car dealer from South London who spent most of his time golfing leaving his fat indolent wife (wives?) to laze around naked on their patio while their prolific blond offspring ran riot round the cultivated lawns and palm trees of San Pedro Del Inglesi, terrorising guard dogs, cats and the gardener Ahmed who one day proudly indicated in sign language to the blond beached whales that he had an equal number of offspring in his home country of Morocco. He might have added that they were being supported on a pittance of a wage that the urbanization tax was comfortably low enough for the beached whales to pay without sacrificing their smiles, suntans or Mercedes.

But back to the more interesting residents. There was old Mr and Mrs Watson at No. 12-'the bookends' as she called them, because of their habit of sitting on their lounge patio day after day at either end of their long dining table which was set permanently outside -in spite of it being antique English yew-neither of them smiling or uttering a single word during this daily ritual but staring straight ahead towards the pool. Food or drink would appear or disappear at the nod of a head or the raising of an eyebrow when one or other of the partners in this idyllic existence would get up and minister to the other. The key to this mysterious, sign-locked language was not even cracked by Brenda in spite of her assiduous application of her binoculars to the unremitting regimen of the Watsons.

Better results were forthcoming when she looked at the doings of Cynthia in No. 15. Cynthia had it all. She had her cake and ate it. She had a town house in Marbella and a boutique to match, she had 'my little pad in San Pedro' with young-but quiescent Spanish lover installed plus two little dachshunds -Schmootsie and Schmitzie. It was rumoured that all four were known to go to bed together on occasions - Brenda knew why and it was her most closely guarded secret except for the details of the death of Betty's last husband Solly. Solly, frankly had been a 'loudmouthed, shit of a man', according to her best friend Doris,' and deserved to meet his maker when he did but not the way he did,' added Delia her twin sister (both ensconced now at No.8), 'even a shit of a man deserves a decent flush into eternity.' But he was drowned and more! Just how much more only Betty knew and would not even divulge to herself except when she had had a few G & Ts.

Then of course there was Jonathan Conyngham-Mortiboys at No. 3. Ex-Anglican priest, ex-hairdresser and now a travel agent based in Hampstead who had built up a flourishing-if somewhat chaotic- business on the back of an enormous knowledge of places, planes, trains and the 'right hotels' coupled with his inimitable gift for personal service - Brenda loved him because he was a match for her culturally and intellectually but she had long since resigned herself to the fact that his body, desirable as it was to her, was 'spoken for' (he always said this in amused whispers). Betty didn't like him because she said, 'He's queer my dear!'. But then Betty's tastes and opinions were simple, stark and unrefined. Bobby, her penultimate husband, a sanitary engineer from Ruislip, whom she had buried only seven years before said she 'lacked breadth and depth except in the 'b-t-m'!'

We must on no account forget George Balls at No. 23-more of him later or Phyllis Lindgrom-the Swedish widow from No.17. But they are just the bit part players in Brenda's winter extravaganza. The summer was for the Essex tribe and their ilk who came and went and whom Brenda kept at the end of her binoculars. The winter was for the ex-pats and the permanent residents or those like Jonathan Mortiboys who came down for long weekends throughout the year. She enjoyed these seasonal digressions spiced up with the Jonathan visitations, it gave a sort of rhythm to her life.

It used to be Trevor who gave the rhythm to her life but after his unfortunate demise she was lost and lacking in drive and direction. All she was left with was a luxurious villa, an ample bank balance, two middleaged sons (Marcus's legacy) whose families only visited for free holidays. Brenda was now 'late sixties', a secret she kept even from herself and had skin 'like an old crocodile handbag' as her youngest perpetually-smiling grandchild was never tired of telling her. But the tears she shed in the early hours were not crocodile tears. She didn't know what they were (posing in front of the mirror in comic detachment, glad eyes up, sad eyes down!) But she got up at seven as she had always done, put her face on, made some bacon and eggs and looked forward to what the day might bring her. She looked in the mirror again, somewhat in awe of herself (raised eyebrows, staring eyes) scrutinised the grand canyons and deserts of her complexion (good bone structure, poor skin) and laughed that raucous laugh that was so constantly mimicked by the younger minions of the Essex tribe!

"It could be worse!" she cackled, "I could be bloody poor as well as old!"

"Cooee! That you Brenda?" shrilled Betty, puffing up the stairs

"Who else you idiot! But I do keep trying to disguise myself"

"Well I hope it's not Jonathan whatsit - in drag!"

"At our age we should be grateful for whatever comes along!"

"You speak for yourself dear -I'm still angling for the ideal toy boy!"

"You disgusting old trout! You're taking me to lunch in Ojen by the way, there's a nice new place opened up there and my foot's playing up and the Merc's on the blink!"

"Your wish is my command!" Betty clowned bowing low.

"What's all this in aid of?"

"My dear you look like the Maharanee of Couch Behar with that towel round your head."

"She can give me her money dear and leave the rest to me! And you can give me five minutes and I'll be down…(shouting down as Betty disappears)..and there's an amusing letter from my 'posh' niece Sarah in the bureau, she's trying to escape from mummy and daddy again!"

GO WRITE THAT NOVEL!

"GO ON," BETTY SAID, "GET it out of your system. Go write that novel. Everyone ought to try at least once in their lives to produce a work of art. Besides, you haven't got anything else to do with your time since you gave up men and stopped coming on holiday with me!"

"I'll try to ignore most of that. Betty Ackroyd, we haven't known each other so long that you can insult me with that kind of patronising nonsense. It won't wash with me! I know I have no literary skill whatsoever beyond what it takes to survive. I can write to solicitors, insurance companies, ex-husbands, but not to a blank wall. I'm no creative artist so please don't fantasise about me. If we are to remain friends!"

That evening Brenda got out her old electronic typewriter which had so long been wasted on household accounts and business letters over the years. She thought of the wealth of experience she had accumulated in the lumber room of her mind and the freedom she now had to sort it all out and convert it into some semblance of artistic order. Not a word came. She crumpled up three sheets of blank paper and then summarily dismissed the typewriter to the magnificent new inlaid bureau she had specially purchased to house it (as though turning the instrument of creativity into a shrine might summon the muse more readily). She felt depressed so she resorted to that other shrine of sympathy -the drinks cabinet (inlaid as well!!). She poured herself the first gin and tonic of the evening. She felt better so she poured herself a second -a big one this time. She sat in her favourite armchair and smiled at the ceiling. She couldn't write like a novelist but by golly she was beginning to feel like one. Then it came to her in a flash, albeit a fuzzy flash, a magnificent title for a novel. She found she was good at titles but less good at following them up. But this title was positively inspirational-'The Ballad of the Fidgeting Buddha' -she could see it all, aided by the binoculars of another gin and tonic.

The story would be about someone like herself, oddly enough, who was trying to be creative and serious but just couldn't get it off the ground. Someone who had retired and was exploring the highways and byeways of what was left of her soul in order to find some semblance of sense. Someone who was perhaps scraping the bottom of the barrel of her life in order to savour the last apples, rotten or not, that had once been kept there -now that sentence will have to go, she said. She was already beginning to write the novel, on the strength of another G & T, but was unable to amend that last sentence, which as you can see still stands in all its pristine overstatedness, to get to the end of this wearisomely long episode -she had mercifully fallen asleep.

Normally by morning she had completely forgotten all the nonsense that may have passed through her mind the previous evening. But this time in spite of a devilish hangover she staggered to her bureau and got out her typewriter and casting caution to the winds began to write....

THE BALLAD OF THE FIDGETING BUDDHA

GOD! SO THIS THIS IS it, is it? Creativity! Well, you can keep it. I've been sitting over this blank sheet of paper for the last twenty seven minutes and nothing has happened. Not a dickie bird! I can't think of anything to write. So here it is. This is my story The story of the unpublished novel. The story that has never been told before. It's the one that got away. Only the clever dicks get through, but 'this time..maybe this time!' (Liza Minnelli singing it), I've cracked it. Well, you're reading it aren't you? No don't put it into the bin yet because the enormities are coming thick and fast and I can promise you that never will your jaw sag like it's going to sag.

Now to business, namely the art of typing from one side of the page to the other without getting bored. I'm getting bored already. So are you. Bit of a failure this. I'd better start a new novel then. Sorry.

Here we go again. Christ., you still here? Mug! Right now for the stylish stuff. 'Somewhat disingenuously he folded the napkin and his sophisticated eyes travelled all the way down from the nape of her neck'… Getting smutty huh? Let's make them travel somewhere else. God knows there are plenty of places to make them travel to. Tee tum, tee tum. Tee tum. Doodling away. There must be something I can write or this story is going to finish right now…………..'

THE SUNDOWNER

BRENDA FELT TRULY PURGED AFTER that bout of literary self-indulgence, which she dubbed her 'creative' phase. She was cured. She had at last owned up to herself that she couldn't write. She was honest. She wasn't one of those fantasising dreamers who always talk about the novel they're going to write when they have the time. She had the time but she couldn't write. Fair enough.

Now cured of artistic pretensions she could concentrate on spending the rest of her life and the rest of her money on the real thing, life. The special pleading tone of her thoughts disturbed her. What was she trying to defend or rather what was she trying to hide from herself? But she was too contemptuous of thought to dwell on the matter for long. It was the dinner after the luncheon after the night before and the light salad and steak coupled with numerous hairs of the dog G & T put her in good spirits to face the night again. She called Betty. Yes, she did want to go to the West Indies but not on a cruise. All that water swirling without and all that Gin and Tonic swirling within would be a combination that wouldn't do either of them any good she said. Besides being on a cruise meant being trapped with the same people for weeks, maybe months on end. It only suited holiday bores who needed a captive audience.

"We've got the money so why don't we roam free. Go to all those fascinating places where they don't have Hilton Hotels?"

"Sounds lovely Brenda. I'm game. But do you think those faraway places are ready for us?" Betty rejoindered.

"They'd better be!" said Brenda, determined to have the last word, "and if they're not we'll wave our magic wands over them!"

SARAH AT SUNRISE

BRENDA HAD NEVER KNOWN SARAH. She was Marcus's niece and she had never known his 'hoity, toity' side of the family. Yet they were to end up in the same place and share a kindred destiny.

Sarah was in her early twenties, twenty two to be exact, and she should be so exact with a huge birthday party looming that very evening. 'Exact', she toyed with the word as she lay in bed, half dreaming and half awake, staring at the canopy of the four-poster. 'Exacting' was a better word. She was dreading it. Her parents were so particular and so resourceful and so burdensomely kind that she felt guilty even thinking these thoughts about them. How could she be so unkind to them to whom she owed absolutely everything from the little bright red 'MG' sports car that had growled its way up the gravel driveway the night before to the wonderful education that had culminated in a B.A. in English, with honours, the previous month.

But that was just it. She felt stifled by all this resourcefulness, this endless provision. She wanted to be angry somehow, but their goodness wouldn't allow it. Her eyes strayed to the vermilion tassels of the fourposter. She tried to count the myriad strands as she had always done since she was fourteen and started thinking about her life. But her intellect wouldn't allow her to, 'a childish syndrome' she mused and then she wanted to shout out very loud for the whole of Penchester Place to hear. But the shout refused to come, it turned into a very loud whisper instead.

"But I'm not fourteen. I'm bloody twenty two going on fifty! She chuckled contemptuously at this first pathetic stab at outrageousness. Then tensed as she heard the quick little click clicks of her mother's slippers as they headed ever so solicitously and ever so inevitably over the polished Elizabethan timbers towards her room.

"Darling! It's quarter to twelve don't you think you ought to get up for lunch. The Dalrymples are coming and they do so want to see you now as they won't be able to come to the party tonight."

Mother was imperious but kind. She was a tall, dignified lady whose presence had graced many a committee room from the highest levels of the Civil Service to the Woman's Institute in their own little village of Penchester. Her large eyes radiated reason and commonsense and it was easy to see how they must have bewitched the young Lord Alfred de Penchester all of thirty years before. But Sarah was beginning to find those self-same eyes resistible. Yet the anger just wouldn't come out.

"Mother, as you can see I'm awake, and I'm gathering myself together to face the onslaught of the Dalrymples!"

"Oh come on darling, they're not that bad, you and Justin seemed to get on so well at the Trinity Ball, that's why."

"That's why you invited those.....those bores without consulting me. Christ mother, I'm not some soppy little Deb at her first coming-out party. This is 1990 not 1950. Give us a break!!"

The anger had come out at last, when it was least expected, as is the fate of all human emotions, and Lady Penchester was hurt, visibly hurt, at her daughter's passionate outburst. As was her wont under such trying circumstances she simply left the room without saying anything. Sarah scuttled into the bathroom and stared at herself in the full length mirror. She looked for signs of the guilt she felt but she couldn't see any. She felt excited too, a little flushed as though on the brink of taking decisions about her own life for the very first time. She tried to look at herself objectively. She was not exactly tall but her elder brother did once say she had 'a nice pair of legs'. Certainly she knew she'd never be as tall as her distinguished mother but she had as her best feature her mother's large intelligent blue eyes and soft fair hair. She daydreamed a little as she showered and dressed. The son of the Nurseryman had once commented impishly, 'You got sexy eyes Miss!' She giggled a little at this and felt a little depressed at how horribly inexperienced she was for a graduate twenty two year old. She was intellectually confident but emotionally and physically she was a chrysalis. She'd had one somewhat dismal 'relationship' in her second year as a student with a nervous Mathematician called Forbes Johnson. But it had all petered out messily at the May Ball when in the early hours of the morning he had fumbled with her behind a holly bush but had been too drunk to get his trousers down properly and she'd been too bewildered and depressed by it all to know what to do. It was then that academic studies became her priority although always at the back of her mind was the thought that one day she might do better than Forbes Johnson.

Breakfast on the North Terrace was a grim affair with mother hiding behind the 'Telegraph' and father who was a man of few words finding even fewer to reconcile the two of them. Sarah nibbled at the toast and was miles away.

Her best pal Lisa was due to fly out to Spain that night to stay at the family villa up in the mountains above Marbella close to where Aunt Brenda lived. She had toyed with the idea of taking up her Aunt's invitation to stay with her but her family had disapproved but then when she had had a second offer from Lisa which she had also turned down, she was beginning to wish she had had a bit more spunk and defied the family embargo. Ahead of her loomed a dreary summer at home with a couple of even drearier weeks at the cottage in Cornwall.

"I'm sorry Mummy! I didn't mean to be so rude to you!" She found herself blurting out.

"Sarah darling! You're just a little overwrought! It's quite understandable! The Dalrymples will be here shortly so why don't you run along and make yourself presentable hm?"

Sarah got up smiling but inwardly wincing and hurried back to the house not to change but to talk to Lisa on the phone.

Lisa would be any girl's ideal friend she was mature and sensible yet at the same time full of fun and good humour. Her people came from the north of England and were big in the travel agency business but they weren't a bit stuffy. Lisa hadn't got Sarah's attractive eyes and hair but she was passable and what she lacked in looks she certainly made up for in a warm and generous nature. She had graduated at the same time as Sarah in Modern Languages and was to take up a temporary post at an International Language School in Estepona in October so her job would be a convenient extension of her planned holiday. She had tried to persuade Sarah to do the same as there was another temporary post going in 'English Conversation' but Sarah had set her heart on a Postgraduate Course at Oxford.

".....to cut a long story short, I've changed my mind 'Lies' (her pet name for Lisa) I want to come with you to Spain...

"Sarah, I'm delighted, as long as you don't mind my brother Martin being with us. You see when you decided not to come with me, I asked him."

"Of course not..the thing is it would be nice to travel out together but I don't suppose I'm going to be lucky with a seat on the same plane at this late hour!"

"We're not flying. Martin's got the Jag and we're motoring down!"

"Oh that's great. Look what time are you starting out?"

The practical details were soon ironed out. She was to drive to Lisa's place that afternoon and Martin would pick them both up later. She packed quickly without alerting suspicions and left a note pinned to the fourposter:

Dear Mummy & Daddy,

Decided to take up Lisa's offer after all. Sorry to mess up all the arrangements. I need to sort my life out and be away from England for a while. Will be in touch later from Lisa's villa. Pass on my apologies to the Dalrymples. I must have just missed them!

Love you,

Sarah

Which indeed turned out to be prophetically true because as Sarah's MG kicked up the dust on the way out through the Lych Lodge Gate the Dalrymples' Rolls was moving sedately in the opposite direction. Once out on the open road Sarah breathed a sigh of relief. It was as if the chains had been broken and she was free at last. It was not that she didn't love her parents but she needed space to grow and breathe.

The journey down wasn't quite what she had anticipated - what she had expected was the cliché of being whisked away into the sunrise by a tall dark and handsome Martin in his sleek new Jag. What actually happened was a long tedious journey through endless pouring rain in a clapped out old Jag that had definitely seen better days. Martin behaved like a fussy old woman and talked endlessly about what was wrong with the car and how he would put it right once they arrived in Spain -if they ever did. However, he was reliable and kind and they did get there in the end after numerous stops. Lisa's sense of humour helped as she was forever poking fun out of Martin's devotion to his car.

The villa was certainly worth waiting for. It was a bright white marble jewel set in the mountains above Marbella. It was in an enclave of such private villas each with their own pool yet arranged around an exotic communal garden pool. From the air it would have looked like a necklace of sapphires and white diamonds. It was called San Pedro Del Inglesi. In the distance could be seen the blue Mediterranean sea and the picturesque little village of Ojen was nearby. She dumped her things and explored. The villa was a good deal less grandiose than she was used to but it was cosy with its own little driveway and carport garlanded with bougainvillea and the whole place was nicely secluded in a lush oasis of a garden teeming full of little flowerbeds and fountains interspersed with squat palm trees. The jasmine- fringed patio looked down on an amoeba-shaped swimming pool with the mountains and the sea in the background.

Lisa and Sarah raced each other to see who would be first into the water. Martin, who couldn't swim, contended himself with unloading and having a last tinker with that gammy camshaft. The two friends lay together on their backs looking at the clear blue sky above, wallowing in the sheer contentment of the carefree month ahead when they could do exactly what they wanted without over-interested relatives planning it all for them.

"Penny for your thoughts!" mused Lisa.

"My thoughts come more expensive than that Lies...God! It's so peaceful here! So where are the men?" giggled Sarah.

"Well, discounting Martin." Lisa giggled, "who has other interests -namely business matters and his car, there are a few to meet, ex-pats and locals etc. We're throwing a housewarming party on Saturday so it should be fun seeing if you can sort out the genuine 'dishes' from the 'creeps'!" Lisa giggled helplessly.

"Oh Lies you are awful! Am I really that naive in your book?

"Just a little green about the gills dear!" Lisa giggled, helplessly and hopelessly, "I'm sorry but I keep thinking of you and that dreadful mathematician at Cambridge. You know! What was his name? Heath Robinson or something!"

"Oh you mean Forbes Johnson!"

"That's him," blurted Lisa shrieking with laughter, "Forbes Robinson, I mean Forbes Johnson."

Sarah drifted nearer to the side of the pool only to find herself staring up into the eyes of Martin who was crouching on his hairy haunches at the side with a tray of drinks.

"Oh my God! You frightened me!" screamed Sarah, Lisa's giggling had moved up a gear and was now positively hysterical.

"It's only Martin, God knows what you're going to be like by the time you meet the rest of the chaps round here!"

"Give it a rest Lisa you've been pulling her leg unmercifully ever since we left England!" said Martin calmly. The girls got out of the water and were towelling themselves down. Sarah couldn't help noticing that Martin was a good deal better looking than she thought with finely chiselled features and, she noted shyly, well-filled pants. He had also noticed her and she felt his dark, searching eyes wandering over her hair, breasts and thighs and giving her body a sensation of warmth and lightness. She felt slightly weak and giddy -the long journey hadn't done her much good and she still felt sticky.

"I think I'll have a shower and get changed before drinks!" she gasped and ran on up.

"It's only Gin and tonic, Ice and lemon until we do the shopping!" Martin shouted after her.

"Oh go and get changed yourself instead of ogling the girl!" Lisa whispered fiercely, slapping him playfully with her wet towel. He did so and as he went inside he pursed his lips and put his thumb and forefinger together in a gesture of approval.

They had dinner out in the Orange Square in Marbella. They were taciturn and subdued -basically exhausted after the long journey and the sleepless nights on the way. It was a humid night and Sarah noted how Lisa and Martin glistened in the candlelight. She noted too how their tanned, handsome and healthy features had much in common -favouring Martin more than Lisa but not unattractive in Lisa. She felt that warm slightly weak feeling come over her again and so she decided to have another drink but Martin was there before her and had filled her glass to the brim.

"Steady on old chap! You don't want to turn her into an alcoholic! We've got another month to go!" mocked Lisa.

"No, no. It's all right! I n-need another drink! Mind you I do feel a bit tipsy!"

"It's an excellent Rose isn't it -we're probably all looking a bit rose to match!" interjected Martin as he filled Lisa's and his own in conspiracy.

"No! That's enough! No more Martin, remember you're driving and we've still got to get the shopping in before the hypermarket closes! I'll settle the bill!" Lisa beckoned the waiter. Sarah was slightly disappointed but knew that Lisa was talking plain commonsense and there would be time enough to let go when they were all settled in and she had found her feet.

It was nearly noon by the time Sarah surfaced the next day. She had been given the master bedroom upstairs which opened out onto a magnificent roof patio with a breathtaking view of the mountains and the sea and all that passed between. She slipped on a bathrobe and ventured downstairs. Martin, who was wearing a very fetching pair of blue shorts and no top, was sitting by the pool under a sunshade sipping a Martini Dry. He looked as though he had been up for hours but there was no sign of Lisa. She felt guilty about this but Martin immediately put her at her ease. She sat in the chair opposite him.

"That's what I like to see! Up at the crack of noon!"

"So what time did you get up then?" she quizzed.

"At the crack of half past eleven as a matter of fact. But I did manage to get changed even so!" He waggled his dark eyebrows roguishly at her bathrobe as he put the conversational ball in her court once again.

"I hope I'm allowed some liberties on the first day of my holidays!" she replied tying the bathrobe more tightly.

"Oh you want to take liberties with me is that your little game!" he said hamming it up delightfully. Sarah laughed and dexterously changed the subject.

"What's happened to Lisa?"

"She's gone into town looking for light fuses. We had a powercut at about half ten this morning. But you and I in our respective beds were blissfully unaware of it. What are you going to drink?" He was flirting with her mercilessly.

"I never drink on an empty stomach and how come you get Lisa to do all the running around for you while you sit drinking the morning away?" She surprised herself at her own bold tone

"Women's lib my love! It's her turn to do the running since I ran the pair of you down here all the way from England!"

While he was saying this he had moved up in front of her, arms akimbo and then fell forward so that his hairy muscular arms held the sides of her chair.

"And when are you going to do your bit of running, hm?" his serious expression suddenly creased into a huge grin. She was so taken by surprise by this that she thought her chair was going to topple over backwards into the pool and so instinctively she dived forward grabbing his shoulders and burying her face in his chest hair. She looked up and surrendered to his smile. They kissed gently at first and then more deeply and insistently. He pulled her blonde hair back with both hands forcing her beautiful face to look squarely into his.

"Please! Let's do it upstairs!" Sarah whispered passionately.

"Sarah!? My you're a sly one! Who would have thought!" Martin carried her up to the master bedroom and they made love quickly and passionately. The floodgates had been opened but just as quickly closed. Martin was nervous that Lisa would return at any time and Sarah needed to find an outlet for her pent-up emotions but didn't find the release her body craved for. She lay back and felt guilty and depressed. Martin said nothing but was surprisingly jaunty after such a brief adventure. He quickly showered and returned to his place at the swimming pool as though nothing had happened. Sarah felt resentful and frustrated. After her shower she calmly dressed went down to the poolside and pushed Martin and his drink into the water and then went for a walk.

She followed a path that clearly led to the village nearby. She had let her blind instincts get the better of her but now her intellect was taking control -a bit late alas. She realised with dismay that she had walked into her first sexual encounter without any forethought or preparation. She had wanted to kick over the traces it is true but she had no idea how sexual passion could work with a relentless will of its own until now. She couldn't believe that she could possibly be so stupid! An ignorant sixteen year old girl without any education would have behaved with more commonsense and dignity!

As she turned a bend in the road whom should she meet up with but Aunt Brenda coming in the opposite direction.

"Oh gosh it's warm and oh gosh it's Sarah! What a surprise! Why didn't you tell me you were coming? You didn't respond to my letter of invitation you little vixen!"

Sarah flung her arms around this 'little heap of flesh' as she had once described her and felt she'd been brought down to earth at last. They doubled back down the road towards the village and had a leisurely lunch in a tiny white-washed hacienda precariously situated betwixt bare mountain and blue sea owned by one of Brenda's cronies from Ojcn. Over the coffee and liquers they poured out their souls to one another.

"Brenda, I can't relate to you as 'Aunt Brenda' somehow!"

"Well I'm certainly not a 'Penchester', if that's what you mean. Your father put paid to that!"

"No I don't mean that. I know my family treated you rather badly after you took up with Uncle Marcus. Pure snobbery of the worst kind too. No I mean..I feel we are like soul sisters!"

Brenda melted a little and took Sarah's hands in hers.

"In spite of everything Sarah, your Uncle Marcus was the only one of my five husbands I ever loved. But he was a bastard. He left me with the two boys to bring up and if it hadn't been for your father's generous allowance in those days I would not have been able to cope. But one of his conditions was that I should abandon my sons and allow them to be brought up by him and his first wife who was unable to have any children of her own. Perhaps I should have said no and struggled to bring them up on my own! I shall never forgive your father for what he made me do nor myself for allowing him to do it!"

"I never really knew my stepbrothers. They sort of disappeared after my father divorced his first wife and married my mother. Didn't Uncle Marcus ever try to get in touch with you?"

"Never! Nor did he show the remotest interest in the fate of his sons! But now I'm financially independent and the boys are grown up, I don't care anymore!"

You still feel bitter about all this don't you?"

"No. 'Bitter' isn't quite the right word. Sarah, a word of advice. Try to keep control of your life.

Never allow anyone to take advantage of you. Now look you must pop off now as I've some advantage to be taking of Carlos my host here -But look I hope to see you at the party on Saturday. Thank Lisa for the invitation."

As Brenda ushered her out she could see Carlos peeping sheepishly through the kitchen hatch.

She was lost in her own thoughts until the hooting of a car coming up the hill brought her back to reality. It was Lisa.

"What brings you out here..Don't tell me! Martin's conversation is enough to drive anyone round the twist!"

"As a matter of fact I've just had a splendid lunch with Aunt Brenda who is coming on Saturday by the way. Martin said you were getting some fuses?"

"He told you about the powercut did he? I wanted to do some extra shopping too for our party on Saturday -only two days to go darling and if you still have your virginity after our little binge you only have your self to blame and we'll be sending you back to Penchester Place lock, stock and barrel with a great royal seal on your fanny!"

Lisa's sense of humour saved the moment, as ever.

"God Lies! What would I do without you? Don't answer that question! And I'm not a virgin!" (which was now technically correct)

"Well stop behaving like one my love. I shall be relying on your sophistication and charm to make Saturday a success!

Lunch was a grim affair, even Lisa sensed there was something up between Martin and Sarah.

"You two had a row or something or what or is it my Greek salad that's not up to scratch?"

"Your Greek salad isn't up to scratch but I think we both must be feeling a little hungover after last night. I could do with some coffee actually!?" drawled Martin mock- arrogantly

"Oh Martin?! Do you want me to draw you a plan of the house and show you where the kitchen is?" retorted Lisa.

"Oh I'll make the coffee Lies, I could do with some myself!" Sarah got up and gave Martin a look as she sidled out.

"That's it feed his male ego and you'll be doing it for the rest of the month!" Lisa shouted after her.

They had their coffee out on the terrace. Martin started plying her with questions about herself and her background and Sarah couldn't help appreciating the irony of the situation. He was asking all these respectful, personal questions after already deflowering her about an hour previously.

"This aristocratic pedigree thing of yours. How far back does it go?" Martin mused twirling his coffee spoon.

"The De Penchesters go back to William the Conqueror I'm told, I'm not really very interested. When you think about it everybody's bloody family goes back to William the Conqueror!" replied Sarah pointedly.

"That's my girl! Martin you should know better. Sarah's sick and tired of answering questions like that and her aristocratic origin is the least interesting thing about her," defended Lisa.

The rest of the afternoon they dozed and after a late dinner on the roof patio the rest of the evening was spent in some spasmodic reading, and indulging in some desultory backgammon, half-hearted chess and a lot of intense Mickey-taking of Martin by Lisa much to the grateful satisfaction of Sarah. He eventually retired defeated to the carport and that gammy camshaft.

"That brother of your is no intellectual, Lies!"

"Six 'O' Levels and an 'A' Level in Economics and Car Mechanics..So he's no professor but he's good to have around when sorting money problems out or the car breaks down!" Sarah could have added other small accomplishments but wisely declined. Instead she suggested to Lisa they go for a swim before retiring. They chatted as they floated on their backs in the delightfully cool water and watched the clear starry sky with its moon and occasional shooting stars. It was heaven. But the thought of the possible consequences of what she had done with Martin abruptly brought her down to earth. She submerged and dived to the bottom, swam the full length of the pool, surfaced and after telling Lisa that she felt tired and wanted an early night, went to her room.

After showering she still felt hot so she took the mattress out on to the roof patio and lay there naked looking at the stars and the full moon. It was indeed a sultry, humid night and she saw that the sweat glistened on her body in the refulgent, milky light of the moon. She felt restless. She arched her thighs and with her fingertips traced the outline of the little golden hairs that lay flat on the backs of her well-rounded calves. She lay flat once again breathing a sigh into the cool night air. She felt the familiar stirring of passion once again, the hot feeling, the slightly sick, sinking feeling in the pit of her stomach and the accelerated thump of her heart. She almost cried out and as if in answer to her prayers he came to her again. He slipped in hard and clean and it was easy for him as she was almost liquid in anticipation of him. His hard hairy hand covered her mouth to stifle the little moans and cries of gratitude that sprang involuntarily from her lips. He was all over her and there was no escape from this wonderful captivity. The second time she was bolder and she was all over him, exploring the mountains and forests and pinnacles of the man's body. She emptied herself of every last reserve and vestige of false dignity. She was licking and sucking him now and he came sweetly in her mouth leaving a little trail of silk from her lips, a silent parody of her greed. They both lay spent until dawn's first light when they were awakened by the chill from a slight breeze blowing from the sea. Together they brought the mattress in and, under the sheet this time, they made love more conventionally but ferociously with Sarah making little begging noises and pleadings- 'fuck me! fuck me! fuck me!'.

By the time the sun was rising Martin had returned to his room and Sarah lay still and satiated, like an animal that has waited a long time for a kill and at last has made it. She felt clean and whole and emptied of all that was unnecessary to her. She felt curiously detached from Martin. She didn't know who he was and cared less. He was a man and that was what she had wanted but now she could dispose of him. This was not what the textbooks said she had to feel. Wasn't it the man who was supposed to be the detached one? Perhaps Martin felt the same detachment, time would tell. But Sarah had moved on and had learnt from the experience. She required a great deal more but Martin would never ever be able to provide it. Nevertheless she was grateful to him for releasing her from the bonds of childhood and adolescence.

When she came down for breakfast there was only Martin on the terrace in his bathrobe drinking coffee. Lisa had apparently gone into the village quite early on another one of her shopping expeditions. The silence was becoming unbearable each one trying to avoid the other's direct gaze.

"Don't you think we ought to talk about it!" Martin mused between sips of coffee. Sarah unleashed a storm of furious contempt that she hardly knew she felt.

"Talk about it! What is there to talk about!? We fuck ourselves silly without so much as a by your leave and without taking the simplest precautions!! I don't know who you are or where you've been and you don't know who I am and what I've done!! Christ!! It's a bit late for talk isn't it??"

"I'm sorry, I thought that."

"Look I'm sorry but being sorry won't help. You'd better give me some reassurances about your sexual history for starters -not that that will be much use!! God! We're a right couple of innocents!"

"Sarah! I'm twenty five but I swear to God you're only the second woman I've ever been with...."

"Oh that's great! Only one other woman to account for! And how many has she been with?"

"It was a girl I used to know in college. She was pretty experienced I admit and had other boyfriends but everytime we made love I used a condom, I swear we did Sarah!"

"That's a relief! Now all we've got to hope for is that I'm not pregnant."

"Sarah! I'm in love with you. Don't you feel any-thing?" She looked across at him as he stared into her eyes like a little lost child. She felt pity for him but not love."

"Oh Martin don't be so melodramatic! What we had was some good sex but not love. It was my first time and that's the truth. I'm grateful to you for 'breaking me in' as it were! Oh God that sounds awful. But fini. That's it. Can't we just be friends so we can enjoy the rest of the holiday without spoiling it for each other and Lisa?"

"I'm not good enough for you that's it isn't it? Lady Sarah de Penchester has not only got lovely eyes, gorgeous legs and soft blonde hair but she's also got an aristocratic pedigree as long as your arm and an honours degree in English from Clare College Cambridge. How can I hope to match that?"

"Oh that's stupid talk! You've got a lot of things going for you but you're not for me that's all. There are plenty of girls out there for you, you just have to get up off your butt and look for them!"

"You really are hard, do you know that? Who would have thought that someone so refined and gentle could be so ruthless!"

"Martin, I don't think there is any point in continuing this conversation. Perhaps I'd better leave the villa for all our sakes! I can always go and stay at Aunt Brenda's!"

"No, for God's sake. Lisa needs you here. Look I'm off to Gibraltar for a few days to sort out some of Dad's business affairs. Perhaps we can talk again about it!"

"About what Martin? There is nothing to talk about. You go to Gibraltar but come back in a sensible frame of mind do you hear?"

He sat staring into his coffee cup and Sarah wondered how she could have been deceived into thinking him such a strong reliable man. He was just an immature little boy masquerading as a man. She felt sorry for him for Lisa's sake.

Violent thunderstorms turned everything upside down for the next two days. The housewarming party was off. Lisa had gone down with a chest infection. Martin, mercifully had gone to Gibraltar, and Sarah had her period just as the storm broke. As the rains came down she ran out on the roof patio and on bended knees shouted to the heavens.

"Oh thank you God! Such exquisite metaphorical timing if I may say so?!"

She raced down to Lisa's room laughing like a schoolgirl.

"Oh Lies I'm so happy! Listen to the thunder! Look at the rain!"

But Lisa was nursing her cold and in no mood for selfish jubilation and she just pulled the duvet over her head and told Sarah where to go in no uncertain terms. A subdued Sarah retired to her room and decided she'd write a letter to her mother. She spent the morning composing it and it reflected her uncertain mood just then. It was full of special pleadings and ingratiating pleasantries and she hated herself for succumbing to such drivel. By lunchtime she had screwed it up and thrown it away. It had stopped raining.

Lisa appeared on the patio swathed in her duvet and sat down looking sorry for herself. She was unusually taciturn.

"I'm sorry for bursting in on you like that Lies! Can I get you some lunch?"

"No thanks I'll only throw up. So what was all the celebration about! Oh yes, Martin's gone to Gib thank God! Yes there is something to celebrate!"

"What are we going to do without the car?"

"He went by hired car, thoughtful man, so we can frolic around to our heart's content. Only I don't feel like frolicking dear! I'm afraid you're going to have to take the car, do the errands and visit my lovely friends without me for a while! I think I could just manage a coffee darling if you're making one!"

Sarah was only too happy to be useful for a change. She felt she'd been taking all the time she'd been at the villa and now she could redress the balance a little.

"So whom do you want me to meet?"

"First things first Sarah, I'm going to smoke my first cigarette since Cambridge!"

"Oh no Lies! You've tried so hard to give it up!"

"No I haven't. I've been lying to you," she lit up and coughed, "and lying to everyone. You know all those early morning visits to the village. Yes?" She dragged and coughed.

"No. Lisa you fraud!" Sarah guffawed loudly.

"I had a hundred quid bet with Martin that I could keep it up until Christmas -I didn't want him to know."

"Well your secret's safe with me, I'm not going to tell you what's good for you -mummy spent the whole of my life until now telling me what was good for me -Martin won't cotton on will he? He doesn't cotton on to anything much!"

Lisa paused, exhaled from both nostrils, and stared silently at Sarah for a while.

"He's keen on you isn't he? Has he tried to…"

"Not only tried Lies, he succeeded!" She had wanted to lie but Lisa's knowing look disarmed her, "How did you guess?"

"I didn't, you just told me you twerp! Oh no -losing your virginity to Martin of all people. He's only just lost his. Couldn't you have waited? -I had so many exciting people lined up for you for whom it would have been a positive pleasure for you to lose your virginity!"

Sarah was refreshed by Lisa's perception and wit but felt a little silly, blurting it all out like that, even to her best friend. She decided to escape to the kitchen for a while.

"I'm going to make myself a steak salad. Are you sure you won't eat anything?"

"Oh no you don't," Lisa spread her legs on to a chair opposite barring the door to the kitchen, "not before you've told me when you did it, where you did it and why you did it!"

At that point the duvet slipped from Lisa's legs. Was it the shock of recognition? Those straight muscular legs were the image of Martin's except they were smooth and tanned and not hairy and white. She cocked one thigh up cheekily and twitched the muscle in her calf. Sarah felt slightly hot and that weak feeling came back. Bodies had that effect on her, male or female, she was very sensual and highly-sexed-she couldn't help being like that but her intensely disciplined upbringing at home and at Convent School had done much to suppress and curtail that side of her. She hardened herself to answer the questions directly.

"A couple of days ago! In my bedroom! And I don't know why I did it. I don't love him -I hardly know him come to that! Satisfied?"

"You are a fool and I bet you didn't take precautions!"

"I had my period this morning!"

"Ah that explains the early morning euphoria! But there are other things to be worried about apart from an unwanted pregnancy aren't there?"

"You're beginning to sound a bit patronising Lies. Look, of course I know what the risks are but it doesn't stop you from taking them when passions are aroused!"

Lisa started one of her giggling fits which was a cue for Sarah to leap over the legs and head for the kitchen. Lisa coughed and spluttered and shouted after her.

"Martin has about as much sex appeal as that piece of uncooked steak you're about to fry! You must have been really desperate!"

"All right then it was 'knee-jerk' sex but what's wrong with that? You're so old-fashioned Lies! Where I went wrong is not taking adequate precautions! I'm hoping Martin's sexual history is not too long and adventurous!" she shouted from the kitchen.

"Adventurous! To the best of my knowledge he's only ever had two women -you and somebody he knew at college! Pamela, what's her name now, Pamela Prendegast. Mind you, she did have a reputation for knowing everybody in the district! Even Martin!"

"Oh my God!"

"What's wrong?"

"I've dropped the steak on the floor that's all!"

"But you'll be pleased to hear that Martin was always obsessed by, and particular about, contraceptives -that is until he met you! I'm feeling lousy Sarah, I'm going back to bed!"

So that was the end of that morning. The clouds that had been building up ominously over lunch presaged the storm that finally erupted in the early afternoon. Sarah was bored and went to bed for the rest of the afternoon and started her holiday reading. She must have dozed off for a few minutes when she heard the front door bell ringing insistently. She looked in at Lisa's room to find that she was fast asleep so she went to see who it was. She opened the little spy door first.

"Ah you're only showing me your beautiful eyes! You must be Lisa's friend Sarah. My name is Kurt and I own the villa just up the hill there. I have some business with Martin but if he's not in I can always call back!"

The bold but impeccably-mannered Kurt was a Danish-born German widower in his late forties who lived at his villa with his elder daughter Anilise for six months of the year and spent the rest of the time running an electronics business just outside Dusseldorf.

"Martin's in Gibraltar we're not sure when he's going to be back. Lisa's not well and she's sleeping at the moment I wouldn't like to disturb her."

"Tell her I'm sorry to hear that she's sick and even sorrier that's she had to cancel one of her wonderful parties. Look Sarah, if Lisa's better by Friday, why don't you both come over for dinner. My daughter Anilise and I would be glad of the company?"

"Oh I'd love to. We've been here over a week and I feel a bit cut off from humanity! Thanks Kurt, I'll speak to Lisa about it O.K.?"

"Until Friday then Sarah. Take care now."

Sarah was indeed glad of the opportunity of escaping from the villa and she wasted no time in telling Lisa when she surfaced around seven. In between coughs Lisa was in buoyant mood.

"Kurt's a sweetie, knows my father very well and he's by no means menopausal so watch your step-mind you, the way you've been behaving lately I think Kurt's going to be the one to have to watch his step eh?"

"He is a little ancient Lies but he does have kind blue eyes that unsettle me somewhat..Now are you going to eat something? You've got to have something to keep your strength up. At least have a soup!"

"You're becoming so disagreeably maternal Sarah -I hope it doesn't augur ill for you!" mocked Lisa, "I'll have that soup!"

The sun returned with a vengeance for the next couple of days making up for its unpropitious disappearance over the previous couple of days. It was unpleasantly hot and humid both by day and by night. But Lisa did shake off that cold and was ready for gadding about again. They had a couple of trips to a private beach that was attached to an exclusive club that Lisa's father had a half interest in but nothing much happened there apart from improving their respective tans. They were both glad when Friday arrived and they could get ready to go to Kurt's place.

The evening was humid and they both dressed in matching silk outfits - wearing as little as they could decently get away with. Lisa wore a figure-hugging blue number with her hair up which made her look older but also accentuated her wonderful figure somewhat and Sarah wore a stunning white outfit with her lovely blonde hair tressed to the shoulders and the Penchester diamond stud- earrings giving that seal of class to the whole picture. Both girls were well-tanned and the golden brown of their shapely limbs was in wonderful animal contrast to the aristocratic cut of the silk.

Together they looked at each other in the full-length hall mirror, astonished at each other's beauty.

"You really have got a wonderful figure Lisa -Do you think we're overdoing it a bit for a small dinner party!?"

"Sarah my darling you not only have a wonderful ass, legs, hair, eyes and everything else I haven't mentioned but those diamonds upstage everything… And Kurt lost his wife two years ago and has only just come out of a bad depression so it'll cheer him up no end to see a right couple of ravers at his door tonight! Especially young ravers and we are unbelievably young are we not?!"

"Lies, I'm going to really miss you when I get back to England!"

They had a hired a taxi for the trip to Kurt's villa because, although it was only a quarter of a mile away, the road was a somewhat tortuous snake that clung precariously to the steep unprotected sides of the mountain. Besides, the taxi driver was a friend of Lisa's father (who wasn't?) and he could be a useful chaperone between villas especially if they had had one too many- Lisa thought of everything!

Kurt met them at the portico of his classically designed villa. He was a wearing a white calf tuxedo with matching trousers and shoes and a red cravat with a large blue stone in the middle, possibly a sapphire. The interior was as sumptuously attired as he was and Sarah began to feel at home and not a bit overdressed.

"You are looking at my sapphire, it's one of the largest you can get and it belonged to my mother. She had Prussian aristocratic connections and they say the sapphire was given by Frederick the Great to one of his mistresses at court and it eventually found its way into our family, legitimately or illegitimately we don't know. My wife used to wear it and I now wear it in memory of her....But I am looking at you! You look so beautiful tonight both of you, welcome!"

He kissed them politely on both cheeks and Sarah felt herself blushing terribly and hoped the tan would hide it, it did! They sank back in the capacious white leather armchairs that seemed to be everywhere and as though on cue the Spanish butler came in with the drinks, ice cold amontillados. A pre-arranged treat for Sarah as it was her favourite pre-prandial.

His daughter Anilise was not in evidence and Lisa enquired about her.

"She is, how do you say in English, indisposed at present, but she hopes to join us for coffee!"

There was a lull in the conversation and Kurt seemed at a loss for words. Sarah suddenly noticed that he was not so confident as his strong masculine appearance suggested. She warmed to him and became quite animated herself almost upstaging Lisa in the conversation. Kurt noticed this too and felt more relaxed as a result. The laughter and talk died down again however when Anilise arrived on the scene -between the dessert and coffee! She was extremely tall and thin and seemed to have very little hair. But her face was very plain and dominated by a huge nose which seemed to have a wart growing out of it that looked like a baby nose emerging from the parent nose, her eyes were small and shifty but shrewd looking. She was dressed very elegantly which almost excused her unprepossessing looks. She was thirty but looked forty. She took an instant dislike to both Sarah and Lisa and didn't hesitate to make plain that fact in hundreds of subtle little ways. She patronised them mercilessly in a disagreeably old-fashioned school ma'amish sort of way.

"You must feel lonely without your parents Sarah. Lisa has got Martin but you really haven't got anyone have you? Andalusia is not the place for a young girl on her own, there are so many temptations and dangers!"

"Oh that's why I like it here!" said Sarah breezily. Kurt laughed heartily at this and his daughter looked daggers at him.

"You enjoy life Sarah and that can only be good!" he said looking seriously into her luscious blue eyes.

"You can still enjoy life without hazarding it I think!" rejoindered Anilise petulantly.

Now Lisa was ready with her broadside.

"You must lead a very safe sort of life Anilise. Don't you think you might be missing out on the (she wiggled her hips suggestively) exciting bit?"

But Anilise wouldn't be thrown, she was an expert at defending herself -having spent a lifetime doing it. And what she lacked in physical endowments she more than made up for in intellectual ones

"My dear Lisa! What some people call excitement is mere self-indulgence to me and pretty shallow self-indulgence at that! Give me the safe excitement of a good book or a classical symphony any day! You can keep the fleshpots!!"

Lisa started to giggle and at once set Sarah off. They couldn't believe this woman. She was not just a frump, she was a parody of a frump! And an old-fashioned frump at that!

"I really fail to see what there is to laugh at!" she said humourlessly, which set Lisa and Sarah into shrieking fits which they now found impossible to control.

Anilise, acutely embarrassed by all this, had had enough.

"Papa, I'm going to bed my headache is returning. If you'll excuse me. Please don't keep my father up too late as he has to be up early in the morning for a business trip to Seville. Goodnight to you!"

"Oh I am sorry Kurt, we've spoilt your evening!" said Lisa calming down now the source of the giggle had disappeared.

"Not at all! Not at all! You mustn't take any notice of my daughter she hasn't been herself since her mother died and she can be, how do you say in English, prickly!"

The two of them were well behaved for the rest of the evening. Kurt was in fine fettle and gave full vent to his knowledge and his wit and the evening passed quickly until interrupted by the punctual arrival of Pablo and the car at midnight.

"Girls! I want to thank you for a wonderful evening, I have enjoyed your company immensely and indeed I am greedy for more..In fact, I know it's short notice, but if you have nothing else to do you can come with me to Seville tomorrow if you like, it'll give you an opportunity to savour the wonderful Andalusian countryside and I could do with the company on the journey!" Kurt was looking directly at Sarah as he spoke.

"Kurt it is sweet of you but I'm expecting a call from Martin tomorrow and I'd rather lie in. But Sarah's not going anywhere!" said darling Lisa.

"I'd love to go Kurt as long as we don't start too early!" Sarah replied eagerly, but not too eagerly.

"We'll have to start around eight as my appointment is around one o'clock. We will also have to stay overnight as it is too much to go there and back in one day. I have my own Hotel in the city centre and a suite of rooms at my disposal but I can arrange for you to stay at a another hotel nearby if you think it more proper!" said Kurt the very model of gentlemanliness.

"I'd love to stay in your Hotel Kurt, thank you!" replied Sarah with no false modesty.

On the journey back they were silent for a while and then Lisa started the giggles.

"Well?" she said attempting to suppress her humour.

"Well what? You're drunk Lisa and you've landed me right in it!" replied Sarah soberly.

"Oh come on! I thought you fancied him? He certainly fancied you!" Lisa was giggling again

"You two were conversationally toing and fro-ing all evening! I barely got a word in, as usual!" Sarah stared ahead.

"But it was you he was looking at darling, or rather your legs, which were sprouting somewhat prominently from under the silk if I may say so!"

"Oh God Lisa you are crude sometimes! He's very nice and well-preserved for a man old enough to be my father and yours! Does every relationship between a man and a woman have to be sexual? I'm happy to do something different on my holiday now let's leave it at that... and stop analysing me! You're becoming more and more like my mother every day!"

"Oh God forbid! I really think you're cross with me aren't you?" Lisa calmed down again.

"Cross? Of course I'm cross! And if you can't get cross with your best pal every so often who can you get cross with?"

"Martin?"

They dissolved into the giggles as the worthy Pablo shepherded them into the villa.

The rolling hills and plains of Andalusia were as magnificent as Kurt had promised and in the already harsh early morning sun they appeared to be the only ones on the long straight road from Ronda to Seville. The endless fields of Olive green trees and sunflowers softened this harshness somewhat and Kurt's gentle retrospective conversation kept Sarah amused and interested all the way. Just outside Seville they stopped off at a cool shady hacienda for an early lunch. Over the refreshing gaspachio Kurt mused awhile:

"Sarah I've been in business over twenty years now and it gets more ruthless and competitive by the day. There used to be rules but not anymore. All right, I'm semi-retired! I've made my pile, as they say. But I don't relish it anymore and I want to return to my first love which is painting -I fell in love with Andalusia when I came here just after my wife died and this is where I want to stay. I love the countryside and I love the people!"

Sarah scrutinised his face as he stared wistfully into the distant landscape. She saw a sad man but a strong man with strong passions. He had wonderful clear blue eyes with just enough wrinkles to make them warm and appealing. He had no double chin and his body looked taut, firm and hard like a young man's. She caught herself blushing as his penetrating eyes suddenly switched to hers.

"I find the landscape somewhat harsh for my rural English tastes but I can see why it appeals to you!" Sarah said, wishing she wasn't revealing so much in her shyness.

"Why does it appeal to me then my little psychologist?" he replied continuing his stare. Her body burned and she felt that telltale weak feeling coming again. His hand covered hers and she felt sure he heard her almost audible intake of breath.

"I..er...I think the landscape reflects your mood of loneliness and austerity..Oh God that sounds pompous!" she giggled and allowed her hand to be enveloped by his completely.

"Sarah you look so beautiful when you smile or laugh and now you are a poet too!" They both laughed until they were interrupted by the presence of the waiter.

The journey to the hotel was now less tense and ominous than she had thought and she looked forward to staying there, her pulse quickened as the Mercedes (the younger brother to Martin's jalopy) pulled up outside the Intercontinental Hotel.

After coffee in the Alhambra Suite Kurt took his leave of her for his business meeting and she went to her room to rest for a while and thumb through a few magazines. She must have dozed off because it was nearly five when next she looked at her watch but Kurt was not due back until six. She showered and oiled herself and lay naked on the smooth satin bedspread. She admired her own body in the mirror above and ran her fingers over her bronzed and curvaceous limbs, over her pert full breasts and the little golden hairs on her thighs and calves, noting the sensuous twitch of muscle in thigh and calf as she raised her legs languorously. It was the way Kurt had made her feel. She had fallen in love with herself through Kurt's eyes. At that moment Kurt appeared at the bedside but she wasn't a bit surprised and saw it as inevitable and natural. She swooned with delight as he undressed and worshipped humbly at the altar of her body which awaited his adoration with such eagerness. His tongue and mouth slopped at the very quick of her and all over her legs and breasts and she gave little quick squeals of agreement as his hands coursed over the very nerves and sinews of her femininity. It was not like with Martin where she hungered for his body, it was his hunger for her body that turned her on. He turned her over and with rough indignity, which she found exciting, took her from behind quickly and decisively.

She had turned yet another corner in the great adventure of the discovery of herself. She lay back content and dozed again. When she awoke she found Kurt lying fast asleep with the instrument of his passion at half mast, but fully sheathed, she noted with a sigh of relief.

The journey back south early the following morning was a subdued affair. Kurt stared ahead at the road and looked vaguely uncomfortable and she felt nothing much. She allowed the colours of the landscape to wash over her and send her into reverie. Once again the familiar harsh browns of the undulating hills and valleys were gently alleviated from time to time by the olive greens and fields of yellow sunflowers. She began to wonder about herself. She pictured herself as a sunflower in such a field, large and strong with life but somehow ugly and a comic caricature of a flower. She felt like a comic caricature of a woman. She'd only been in Spain a matter of a couple of weeks and she'd had sex with two quite opposite types of men without any real feelings about it at all except animal satisfaction. Perhaps she was a whore, a harlot, a strumpet, a trollop,…. the myriad euphemisms for prostitute came thick and fast into her consciousness. But her trained and intelligent mind quickly dismissed the ramblings of her superego as one last attempt by her absent mother to subdue her. Nevertheless she couldn't subdue the speculations that kept coming. Maybe she was ill, maybe she was warped in some way?

She was woken from her reverie by the swirl of gravel as Kurt's Mercedes drew up in the driveway of his villa.

"I thought we'd agreed that you were to drop me home?" said Sarah with more venom than she had intended, "look I'll walk the rest of the way, I need some fresh air!"

Kurt gave her a sort of hangdog look and said:

"I'm sorry Sarah! I thought there was something more between us than apparently there was. I'm a silly old fool!"

"No you're not! I hope we're going to remain friends and I hope to see you soon!" replied Sarah giving Kurt a great deal more confidence than he had merited, "and thanks for a wonderful trip across Andalusia!"

She felt relieved to be by herself again and the walk back down the road was mainly in the shade so she could relax and wind down a little. She was beginning to feel good about herself again and even began to hum a tune she had heard some gypsy beggars singing outside a Bodega in Seville. As she rounded the bend of the road and into the driveway of her villa she suddenly stopped at the scene confronting her. Two police cars were parked at oblique angles to the front door and a man in plain clothes was standing between them talking into a walkie talkie. She found herself running the rest of the way and when she got in through the open doorway the hallway looked like a comisaria de policia. Lisa was sitting down on the couch sobbing her heart out and when she knew Sarah was there she jumped up and threw her arms around her.

"Oh Sarah! Martin's been killed in a road accident on the N347! And there's more, the police found a quantity of drugs and other things in his car! Oh God! What are we going to do!? What are we going to do!?"

Sarah gently led her into the lounge. So numbed was she with shock it was easy for her to console Lisa and she remained in this detached state until all practical natters had been taken care of. The police had been persuaded to come back the following day having been reassured that no one was likely to do a midnight flit. But they insisted on posting a plainclothes man at the end of the driveway -one of the men with the walkie talkie, the fat one. She had got in touch with Giles Barrington, Lisa's father, and he was flying out that afternoon. Piers Rambard, the family solicitor would be coming from a nearby villa later on. It was about four by the time she fixed herself a martini and settled down to catch her breath. Lisa was mercifully asleep -the double scotches had done the trick. Sarah sat and stared into space, a light wind was gently playing with a loose lock of her golden hair but she was too stunned to put it in place. Shock gave way to some grief-not for Martin, curiously enough, but for Lisa. She found herself crying for the first time in a long while. She felt lonely. She was crying as much for herself as anybody else. But grief soon gave way to fear. The refrigerated brain was thawing out and she was beginning to think things through. Why did the police need to leave the man with the walkie talkie? It was obvious. The drugs connection was a sinister threat that made her go cold. Perhaps the police thought she and Lisa were in on it or maybe there was something more ominous in the police presence, maybe they were in danger from the drug runners and their accomplices. She felt lonely and afraid and wished that she had played it safe and stayed in Penchester Place. She felt a hand on her shoulder and gave a jump. But it was only Lisa who was looking more composed. She sat silently next to Sarah, nursing another double scotch.

"Whisky certainly eases the pain. I just can't believe it Sarah. I know he was a bit of a pain in the arse but he was my brother. I don't know how he came to be mixed up in drugs. He would have told me if there'd been any trouble -he never kept anything back from me you know?"

"But you did say he went off on those business jaunts rather a lot and you didn't know precisely what it was that he got up to!"

"Sarah! He worked for my father. It was all hotels, package tours, holiday arrangements. He was away rather a lot, Morocco and Tunisia mainly, but he had no reason to get into drugs, he had no money worries..no worries of any kind that we knew of."

They got sloshed together and it was only the urgent ringing of the front door bell the following morning that woke them, or rather, her -Lisa was still dead to the world. Sarah rose stiffly from the patio relaxer, that she'd obviously ended up on the previous night, and staggered balefully to the door which rang again just before she opened it. It was, not unexpectedly, the fat plainclothes policeman with the walkie talkie. He spoke Spanish with a Catalan accent -Sarah's Spanish was that good- and whined about his predicament of having to 'guard the ladies' all night long without so much as a coffee to keep him awake and that he'd appreciate one now. His fat jowls needed a shave and she felt revolted at the sight of all that sweat over all those chins and the unsuccessful efforts of his podgy hand plus hankie to disperse it. She felt like telling him that since his night duty was over there was no need for him to have any coffee to stay awake -he could sleep to his heart's content, but instead she asked him in.

"You speak Spanish good, lady!" he said in faltering English, "You call me Alphonso do you hear?"

Mercifully Lisa appeared on the scene. She told Alphonso in no uncertain terms that they were not dressed yet and that he was to remain on duty outside until his superiors arrived. She ushered him unceremoniously out of the villa.

"I can see why you're so popular with the male sex Sarah! You are so naive sometimes and yet you have the wiles of a witch! Pass me that packet of Gauloise on the bureau I need a cigarette!"

"Oh for Christ's sake Lies!? I was just offering him some human hospitality -he's been on duty all night- and you interpret it as making a pass at him!? Do you think I'm so desperate that I'd go for someone like that?"

Lisa started to giggle and Sarah joined in until they were almost hysterical and then they calmed down just as unexpectedly. Lisa lit her cigarette and took a long cool drag.

"It's just the sight of you offering respectable hospitality in decidedly unrespectable skimpy silk pantaloons that creases me!" With that the hysterics started again.

"Best be quiet so we don't wake our guests!" hushed Lisa.

"What guests??"

"Well you invited them but you were dead to the world by the time they arrived, about two o'clock.... My father and Piers Rambard of course!"

When Lisa's hysterics finally subsided they turned into tears and as if by osmosis Sarah too wept. All cried out they had breakfast in silence on the terrace. It was going to be a hot day but there was a gentle breeze and Sarah found this comforting. She lay back and enjoyed the early morning sun, closing her eyes and playing the languorous game of anticipation..anticipating the movements of the breeze gently coursing across her face, anticipating in wild reverie the potential of the unknown forces around her, the drug barons, the unshaven police and Lisa's guests lying dormant in the rooms above.

Sarah must have been asleep for some time because the sun was high in the sky by the time she surfaced to the sound of male voices raised in anger. Sarah peeped through the terrace window to see what looked like a reprise of yesterday's comisaria de policia scene. The fat walkie talkie was standing in the doorway and two more important looking uniformed policemen appeared to be arguing with Lisa's father. Giles Barrington was a very large, silver-haired, distinguished looking man who looked as though he could play with the short Spanish policemen like you'd play with marionettes and he was clearly angry but keeping it under control whereas the Spaniards gestured wildly with Latin theatricality. Lisa sat on the couch holding Piers's hand and looked stunned. She made her entrance.

"Piers take Sarah and Lisa out into the garden, I'll deal with this!" said Giles with authority.

They sat in a little arbor of bougainvillea near the South wall which had an excellent prospect of the sea. They didn't speak for some time.

"Do you want to tell Sarah or shall I?" said Piers bluntly, coiffing back his thick blonde hair and staring nervously at the ground.

Lisa stared into the distance and drained of all emotion said:

"It seems to be getting more complicated all the time. Apparently, they now seem to think that Martin was not killed accidentally. They think he was murdered. The car crash was just a consequence. They found two bullet holes in the side of his neck! They want us to go down to the comisaria de policia in Marbella to answer a few questions!"

"Do they think we're mixed up in it?"

"They say its just routine! Oh God!"

"There's nothing to worry about believe me, we have plenty of good Spanish contacts to see our way through all this!" said Piers unconvincingly, "But we have to be wary of the press, we're going to try to keep your name out of it Sarah. If they ever knew you were the daughter of Lord Penchester the tabloids would have a field day! I've had to tell your father too. He's coming over as soon as he can get a flight out!"

Sarah was beginning to feel frightened. She had just began to feel that she was in control of her life and now she felt she was being dragged down by a great dark tide that threatened to engulf her forever.

They huddled into the tiny comiseria just above the orange square in the old town, cheek by jowl with a couple of disdainful prostitutes and a Swedish couple who'd had their passports stolen. A uniformed officer was two-fingeredly picking out a report on a battered Remington and the monotonous noise together with the heat and the claustrophobic atmosphere caused Sarah to feel most peculiar and she promptly fainted. When she recovered she found them all peering down at her as she lay on a stretcher in what looked like one of the cells.

"Thanks Sarah! We're being attended to straight away, much to the chagrin of the two old whores! Are you feeling better?" said Lisa seemingly back to her usual humorous self.

Sarah could only manage a smile and accepted the glass of iced water proffered by Piers, courtesy of Marbella Police.

The ordeal only lasted about an hour with Lisa and Piers doing most of the talking. The police seemed very respectful of Sarah once they realised that she was of an aristocratic background. They seemed to be convinced that she had nothing whatsoever to do with Martin or with the people he may have been doing business with and that she was just a friend of

Lisa's. Unfortunately this wasn't the end of the matter. The police were equally convinced that Lisa was under threat, and so was Sarah by association. They were advised to leave the country and until such time as they did they would be provided with police protection to the tune of one armed plainclothes officer with a walkie talkie -Alphonso would be getting that cup of coffee after all!

Out in the glorious sunshine they made for the orange square for an early lunch. They sat in the shade near the fountain and collected their thoughts.

"This whole affair smells!" Lisa said adamantly.

"You're right Lisa, it's a coverup! I think there's much less to all this than meets the eye." said Piers authoritatively.

"Less?" Lisa raised a quizzical eyebrow.

"Piers is right Lies! It's obvious the police are covering something up that's why they are laying it on thick and fast, police protection etc, trying to get rid of us. It would be more natural for them to want to keep us here as bait for these drug people!" said Sarah, coolly airing her intellect for the first time since Cambridge. Piers had that effect on her. He hadn't got quite the same physical charms as Martin had, he was a little too thin for her tastes, but she was excited by him and the combination of his sharp mind, straight nose and penetrating blue eyes brought on that slightly weak feeling again.

"I have an address..Martin left it with me in case of any emergencies before he went to Gibralter." Lisa whispered.

"An address? You never mentioned it before Lies!" replied Sarah, somewhat surprised and once again reminded of the close bond that existed between Martin and Lisa.

"We have to follow this up. There are risks but for Martin's sake at least we need to disentangle this mess and get to the truth!" said Piers quietly and undramatically.

"It's all very well for you two to play the detective game! We could very well end up as a meat sandwich between the police and the drugs lot and frankly I'm too exhausted to think about anything else but the funeral tomorrow...I want to go home Lies!" pleaded Sarah. Lisa too was looking vulnerable again and Sarah allowed her to rest her head on her shoulder. Piers got up and paid the waiter, throwing a conspiratorial wink at Sarah. They drove back to San Pedro in silence.

A few days later, with little ceremony and few guests, Martin's ashes were interned in the flowered wall of a small cemetery in the picturesque village of Ojen. Sarah comforted the weeping Lisa but felt strangely detached. She just couldn't make the traumatic connection between the strong physical body of the Martin she knew and the little urn of ashes at that precise moment being placed in the wall by the local priest. Her attention wandered. She wondered what shape the priest's legs were and whether they were as hairy as his hands. Her gaze met Piers's and she felt herself blushing. She reflected on the surrealistic warp and woof of existence that enables such irrationalities to blend together quite happily with the banalities of everyday relationships. At the dramatic moment when the urn was cemented into its final resting niche, Lisa clenched Sarah's hand and with the tears coursing down her cheeks, cried out:

"For God's sake find out who did this to Martin!" she turned to face Sarah, "I'm counting on you Sarah!"

"Oh Lies! Lies!" was all Sarah could muster as she embraced her. Leaving it to Piers to give coherent shape to her intentions.

"We won't rest until we have got to the bottom of this mess and completely exonerated Martin! Trust us!" said Piers.

He's decided that we are a team then, thought Sarah. She felt a little piqued at this presumption, bordering as it was on impertinence, but the weak feeling came back and she accepted it without demur. But one thing she was certain of and that was, come hell or high water, she would do her utmost to uncover the sordid realities of this tale, with or without Piers. She had found a new purpose and resolve in her life and she wasn't going to let go of it as easily as she had let go of her lovers.

The address on the back of an old electricity bill read, '34 Old Ship Street, Gibraltar'-there was no name or message of any kind, but Lisa was adamant that that was the address Martin gave her on the day he had departed to Gibraltar for ever.

It was a blustery, quite cool day as they passed through Passport Control and along the long concrete road that joins the island to the mainland with the aircraft landing strip at right angles to it. They had an early lunch at an English pub, English except for the fact that it was run by Gibraltarians who were very voluble and anxious to communicate and were full of local gossip. They certainly knew where Old Ship Street was although they seemed wary and somewhat surprised when they knew that they had 'friends' there.

Outside the pub Sarah expressed her delight at the obvious friendliness of the pub clientele.

"I think most of them are 'gay' darling, and the one in the earring obviously fancied me! But rest assured the feeling wasn't mutual!" said Piers flushed after three scotches.

"I had my suspicions. I may have led a some-what closeted existence hitherto but my sexual litmus paper never lets me down." purred Sarah eyeing him sideways.

"I like it! I like it! But 'Closeted'? A wrong choice of word darling, it doesn't become you -Leave it for those living in the closet!" with that Piers hustled her across a narrow street and into a waiting taxi. Piers was a great one for hustling and bustling away and in general not standing still for more than a minute at a time. But Sarah was warming to him and was excited at the thought of not knowing from one moment to the next what he was going to do. He was a great change from the predictable men that she had been lumbered with all her life from her father onwards.

Old Ship St was indeed Old but not terribly shipshape. It was in the least salubrious quarter of 'the rock' and it was with some trepidation that Sarah watched the familiar taxi take off leaving them in a dark and unfamiliar alleyway which appeared to lead steeply up the side of 'the rock' itself. But Piers blustery humour calmed her. She felt safe with him somehow, in spite of his impetuosity, or maybe because of it.

'Number 34' was somewhere near the top of the street. It was a grey shabby sort of terraced house indistinguishable from lots of others in the locality and it appeared to be empty as there were no curtains on the windows and from what could be seen of the rooms they looked vacant. But on pressing the bell there were signs of life and activity. Someone looked out of an upstairs window and someone else could be heard trundling down the uncarpeted stairs. A thin youth in a towelling robe and black boots sheepishly opened the door and stared at them. He couldn't have been more than thirteen or fourteen and didn't appear to know English or Spanish. Piers tried French with more success.

"Ah oui! Mon ami est ici! Attendez s'il vous plait!" Sarah and Piers looked at each wondering who to expect next as the boy trundled back upstairs, leaving them to peer through the half-open door at a very bare hallway and a naked lightbulb hanging dutifully from the cracked ceiling. The next thing took them completely by surprise. There was the sound of voices and Sarah jumped in surprise, she knew who it was.

Kurt appeared at the door and was also wearing a towelling robe and was just as surprised as the others.

"Sarah! Piers! How lovely to see you both! But what brings you here?"

"We might just as well ask you the same clichéd question Kurt!" Piers rejoindered.

Kurt stood somewhat dumbfounded for several seconds looking first at Sarah and then at Piers.

"Would you rather talk to us here or do you want us to come back later?" Sarah suggested, trying to break the ice with as small a metaphorical pickaxe as she could find.

"I think you'd better come in!" said Kurt resignedly.

"I think we'd better!" said Piers.

Kurt led them up the reverberating stairs to a dark corridor that led to a green baize door which opened on to another door on the other side of which was the most sumptuously furnished apartment that one could possibly imagine outside a royal palace. There was no sign of the boy that had appeared at the door who by this time must have ensconced himself in one of the rooms nearby judging by the shifty nervous backward glances that Kurt kept giving.

He bade them sit down and offered drinks, an offer which was as speedily declined by Piers.

"I suppose you got my address from Martin. I can't tell you how sorry I was to hear about the tragic accident. That N347 is a killer and no mistake."

"Kurt, you can't believe that. Even the papers are now reporting the murder investigation!" said

Sarah quietly, "Why did Martin arrange to come here that Saturday? He never told us it was your flat he was going to visit, he said it was just business."

"You will recall we were in Seville then!" replied Kurt coldly. At that point the youth they had met earlier came in carrying a tray of coffee cups etc. He was fully dressed this time wearing a tight fitting light-blue silk shirt and well-cut white trousers that Sarah thought were so fetching that she almost lost her train of thought.

"Oh by the way this is my son -my adopted son from our time in Toulon. Guillaume. He speaks little English but he is at home in Spanish or French. He is sixteen and to spare him the strain, languages not being his good point, I'll offer you his delightful coffee!" muttered Kurt

"Merci Guillaume, merci beaucoup!" Sarah accepted with an alacrity that discomforted Piers and he was forced to accept too but he didn't forget the train of thought. He also noted Guillaume's wide-eyed smiling grin at Sarah.

"Kurt it's not really a courtesy call, we are trying to find out as much as we can about Martin. Lisa wants to clear his name and to get to the truth of the matter. Maybe there are things that you don't want to tell us but all we want to know is what exactly was Martin up to that caused him to die the way he did. You must know something!"

"Who sent you! The police?" said Kurt curtly.

"No. This is a personal matter Kurt. Lisa asked us to clear Martin's name. As a matter of fact the police have asked us to leave the country. They are afraid for our safety," said Sarah.

Kurt went over to the window and looked down into the street below. He was nervous. He wasn't the man that Sarah had dinner with and the man with whom she'd had sex in that hotel in Seville. He seemed smaller and more frightened.

"Martin and I did business together. I knew his father quite well. We'd been students together at the L.S.E. in the mid fifties and we met up later in Marbella. As you may be aware Martin acts for his father a lot of the time and promotes his business interests in this part of the world...."

"Could you just cut the crap Kurt and get to the point!" said Piers impatiently.

"I'm just trying to fill in the background first. Martin did get involved in a lot of risky, fringe activities that I knew of but didn't get closely involved in myself."

"Such as?" chipped in Sarah.

"To be brutally frank! He was being blackmailed!"

"Well, spit it out then. We want the whole truth for Lisa's sake!" interjected Piers. Kurt looked shocked. He looked first at Piers and then at Sarah as though playing for time, gathering strength to say what he had to say.

"Sarah, it's going to be awfully difficult telling you this and a considerable risk to myself and my nearest and dearest and that includes you!"

"Kurt you must tell us the truth. Please!" Sarah said softly, she felt weak.

"I'm afraid it's your Uncle Marcus. He is Mr Big, the man behind the whole of this tangled mess!" Kurt sat down staring into space. Guillaume put his hand on his shoulder with all the tenderness of a young lover. At that moment Sarah intuited the nature of the relationship and the possible nature of the blackmail. Yet she and Kurt had had sex! But her mind was racing beyond this to the inevitability of what followed from the Uncle Marcus saga..Her life too could very well be in danger. She clung tightly to Piers as Kurt continued to unravel the tangled mess.

"Your Uncle Marcus always was a clever man Sarah but an unscrupulous one too. He was a finance chap with some West Indian Sugar companies in the sixties and then got mixed up with some business people in Guatemala and ended up working for drugs cartels there and elsewhere. About ten years ago he started up his operations here in Southern Spain and in Gibraltar. He is very discreet but quite ruthless with those he considers to be his enemies and both myself and Martin fell into that category. I bitterly regret the joint business ventures we entered into, nothing to do with drugs I can assure you, but I did find myself at the thin end of Marcus's money laundering schemes with no way out but either to cooperate or go under. I am now at the dangerous stage of non-cooperation!"

"What part did Martin have in all of this?" queried Piers.

"Martin was just a small-time drugs courier who got caught in the crossfire as it were. That's why the police have been so cagey by the way, they're on to Marcus and want to catch him but they're not quite sure whether in the crossfire it was their bullets or Marcus' that did the deed."

"Oh my God! Kurt that explains a great deal! Oh what am I going to be able to tell Lisa? I'm so sorry! Uncle Marcus abandoned his own family but we had no idea he would come to this! And Aunt Brenda still loves him!" Sarah wept unashamedly.

"Oh come on Sarah, we've got to see this through!" comforted Piers, stroking her hair and letting her head rest on his chest.

"Sarah, you've no need to feel any guilt. I'm so sorry you've been let down this way. Let me get you both a drink," Kurt motioned to Guillaume to get the drinks trolley.

"No thanks Kurt. We'd better be on our way back to San Pedro and to Lisa." said Piers brusquely as he shepherded Sarah out.

"Piers and Sarah be circumspect, many people's lives are at stake here and one false move could mean disaster for all of us. We're all in your hands now! If there is anything I can do to get this man put away I'll do it, don't hesitate to let me know!" said Kurt emotionally but Piers didn't take his extended hand as he and Sarah went out into the Gibraltar night.

They were exhausted and decided to spend the night at the New Anchor Hotel before returning to Marbella. Tearful and remorseful, Sarah was grateful for the no-nonsense sex that she and Piers had that night under the shadow of the rock. But it was pure escapism and she felt as purged and empty as she had before with Martin. Piers must have felt the same way because they said absolutely nothing to each other on the whole journey back to Marbella.

On the way up the steep mountain track to San Pedro Piers broke the silence.

"We've got to tell Lisa the truth, we owe her that. While you were asleep this morning I was on the mobile to your father putting him in the picture. He is aware that the British consulate have to be involved and we must get things moving quickly on our side before the Spanish authorities are involved.

"Oh Piers what am I going to tell Lisa!" Sarah whimpered. Piers eyes blazed at her, "For God's sake grow up woman! She's your best friend. Marcus is your uncle. You are going to have to tell her. I'm dropping you off here at San Pedro."

"Don't leave me Piers!" she shrilled hysterically.

Piers slapped her hard across the face. She stopped crying and just looked open-mouthed at him.

"I'm doing my damndest for you but you've got to play your part too. I'm leaving you here to tell Lisa what's happened and keep her company whilst I go back to Estepona where you father is with some important people who can help us. We'll contact you by phone and we should both be back at the villa by midnight."

As they rounded the bend of the mountain track they were greeted by a blazing, noisy San Pedro Del Inglesi -there were festoons of coloured lanterns everywhere and the taut accordian rhythms of an Argentinian tango reverberated about the place.

"A party! Well that should take your minds off things for a while!"

"Piers, at least come in for a while. I don't think I can face all these people on my own!" said Sarah.

"You can and you must. I'll see you later!" with a brief smile Piers drove on. Daunted by his seeming indifference to her distress she stared for a moment at the majestic velvet sky with its scattering of diamond stars equally indifferent to her and the vulgar sights and sounds below. Then she picked up her valise and went in.

There were lights on in the villa so she knew that Lisa was in but it took her some time to get to the door

THE WITCHES'
CAULDRON

"WELCOME HOME STRANGER! I'VE GOT a guest I want you to meet!" garbled Lisa. She had obviously had a few but not quite drunk yet, judging by the steady hand that proffered the champagne. It made Sarah's job a lot easier.

"I want you to meet (she sang the next bit like a fanfare of trumpets) Dandaran daran dan dan dan dan! Jonathan Conyngham-Mortiboys from No.3! This is Sarah De Penchester my bestest friend ever!"

"Just call me Johnny dear -everyone here does. Pleased to make your acquaintance 'bestest friend ever'. We are having a big party tonight to celebrate the birthday of one of our longest standing residents here at San Pedro Del Inglesi- Brenda Elizabeth Barratt no less from No. 1. We couldn't get in touch with you to give you advanced notice but we hope you'll accept our invitation just the same. There's loads of food wine etc laid out in the communal garden, courtesy of the urbanisation committee and we've got an Argentinean group 'Noches de Tango' to entertain us. So..this is Sarah de Penchester. Sweetie you look lovely but I must trot along (he whispered) cos we're needed in the garden!" he clasped her hands briefly and then disappeared through the patio door to the assembled throng dragging Lisa in his wake.

Sarah showered put on a bathrobe and was going to sink into her bed to brood and sleep. But she wasn't so tired as she had thought. She slipped into the white silk dress and put on the Penchester diamond-stud earrings which she wore to such great effect at Kurt's dinner party. She went to the mirror and gorged herself on her own reflection and that together with insistent whines of the tango accordion served to reinvigorate her. Sarah suddenly felt better, drained her glass, refilled it at the bar and joined them outside. She melted into the anonymous throng until drawn out again by Johnny who whisked her to the very heart of the tango -she was sent into a delirium by the insistent thump of the beat and the other dancers made way for them as they took the floor in La Camparsita, El Choclo, etc. Johnny was a wonderful dancer and sensitively anticipated her every move with exquisite timing - they got a little applause at the end of their 'exhibition' dancing, as Lisa later called it. It was a humid night but a gentle breeze played on the glistening bronzed faces of the happy throng. Johnny introduced her to their other competitors on the dance floor Gerald and Barbara Watson from No.12.

"Oh we're not in your league dear -We're more your 'Come Dancing' Tango"

"I thought you were very good!" Sarah lied. Johnny whisked her away again.

"Brenda calls them the 'bookends'.... which reminds me you must now meet your Aunt Brenda, the Queen Bee of San Pedro Del Inglesi, in whose honour this little gathering has been arranged. She is looking forward to seeing you again."

She was standing with Betty near the barbeque fire talking animatedly with Lisa. She too was wearing white with a stunning diamond encrusted choker.

After the formalities the group took their food and wine down to a small garden alcove down by the pool which had comfortable banquettes and was sufficiently private but not cut off from the main hub of the party.

"You're a wonderful looking girl Sarah -You too Lisa! If Betty and I had either of your looks at your age we'd have each had ten husbands instead of five!"

"I think I'd have settled for just one good one who could have stayed the course dear!" said Betty.

"Well, to tell you the truth.....Sarah and I have just been experimenting with men..Oooh I feel a bit giddy!" Lisa slurred, smiled wanly, then collapsed.

"Experimenting with men! More like experimenting with drink dear! Come on Johnny let's get her back to her villa!" said Betty matter-of-factly.

"And don't forget to come back you two. The night is still middle-aged!" Brenda shouted after them and then added, "even if some of the partygoers are old!" She then turned to Sarah who was staring at her intently, burdened as she was with the knowledge that Kurt had imparted. "Sarah, why are you staring like that? You look as though you've seen a ghost. I think like Lisa you're tired and maybe you've had too much to drink…"

Sarah cut her short.

"No, no. I can hold my drink. I was just taken aback by what somebody had told me about…."

It was at that point that it was Brenda's turn to blanch, She stared ahead over Sarah's shoulder with a startled, incredulous expression on her face.

Johnny, Betty and Lisa returned with an uninvited, surprise guest for Brenda. At this point a waiter wheeled out the birthday cake which was a forest of flaming candles and sparklers and everyone gathered around.

Johnny made the introduction in his hollow theatrical way which didn't quite suit the occasion alas.

"Brenda Barratt -Meet again your first husband Marcus, who wishes to greet you after forty two years in the wilderness and wish you a happy birthday!"

There was an awkward silence broken only by the hissing of the sparklers as the white-suited figure of an elderly man stumbled forward in the semi-darkess to plant a kiss on the numbed cheek of Brenda. A neutral observer might be forgiven for thinking that this was the Garden of Gethsemane revisited. Sarah stood nearby shaking with shock and fear.

"Happy birthday to you! Happy birthday to you! Happy birthday dear Brenda! Happy birthday to you!" They all chorussed.

"It's been a long time Brenda. I've got a sort of present for you. It's a sort of peace offering if you like -'Least said soonest mended'!" Marcus's voice had grown huskier over the years.

He held out a small neatly wrapped box. She opened it and she gazed with wonderment at the large blue stone which seemed vaguely familiar to Sarah and Lisa.

"Oh it's beautiful -Marcus! I'm not sure whether we can forget.... but we can certainly forgive after all these years.. I'll have to have it set in something. It's a sapphire isn't it? It's really beautiful."

"Yes. It's apparently one of the largest sapphires you can get. It's got Prussian aristocratic connections and they say it was given by Frederic the Great to one of his mistresses at court and it eventually found its way to me!"

"Look, friends. Thank you for tonight. But you'll have to excuse us, Marcus and I have got a lot of catching up to do after forty years!" There was a strange emotion in Brenda's voice which Betty and her friends couldn't really comprehend. Brenda always put up a detached and witty front to life. It was unusual to see her looking so vulnerable. The assembled throng gave a gentle applause and quietly dispersed leaving Marcus and Brenda to return to her villa arm-in-arm. Johnny Mortiboys stared after them.

Sarah and Lisa looked at one another in mute recognition and mutual horror. The two of them slipped away behind a nearby palm tree. The strong coffee had had the desired effect on Lisa and she was more her composed self. Sarah now had the courage to tell Lisa the whole story of Gibraltar.

"I had no idea he was your uncle. How could this bastard be so brazen! Oh God! We must inform the police straight away!" was all Lisa could say amid her choked back tears.

"We mustn't act precipitately Lisa. Dad and Piers have got things in hand and Piers promised he'd be back late evening. He could be back at any time. Let's just go back to our villa and wait."

As they walked back with their arms round each other shots rang out from one of the villas. It was from Brenda's villa.

"Oh no! He's shot Brenda now!" The two women ran to their villa in a state of hysteria and in the pitch darkness cowered under the stairs. Johnny had been first on the scene in Brenda's villa. He found Brenda staring into space with a large smoking pistol in her hand. Marcus lay in a pool of blood with half his face blown away -eyes pointing comically in two different directions. Johnny tried to do something but it was clear that Marcus was well and truly dead. All Johnny could do was look up at Brenda and say:

"Oh Brenda darling where in God's name did you get that gun?

She paused for a moment and then still staring in the same direction replied calmly:

"Oh it was his gun. I don't keep guns. He was showing off with it saying he had enemies. I'll say he had enemies. I knew all along that sapphire belonged to Kurt. I can imagine how he got it off him too -Kurt promised it to me you know. He went to pour himself a drink near the patio and left me with the gun. I thought if I aimed just below the left shoulder blade near the spine the bullet would penetrate his heart and he would die instantly. But then all of a sudden he turned round and asked me whether I wanted a G & T -He remembered I enjoyed a gin and tonic. I faltered for just a moment, I could have spared him. But I think it was the smug smile on his face that finally did for him. I shot him in the face as many times as I could while he was still standing. Only two bullets got him in the chops, the others look as though they've ruined my chaise longue!" Brenda giggled, cackled and then broke down in sobs.

The police arrived within minutes and cordoned off the area, keeping out the gawping crowds -They were led by Sarah's father, Piers and the two grim-faced officials from Estepona.

"Where is my daughter and her friend?" shouted Lord De Penchester imperiously at no one in particular.

"They went to their villa I think sir!" Johnny whispered, "Ill take you there!"

"No you won't," said one of the grim faced men, "You're needed here my friend."

Piers and a police officer took Sarah's father to the villa. After a good deal of pounding on the door Sarah and Lisa let them in. They looked like two frightened white mice.

"How on earth could a well-educated daughter of mine get mixed up with this," he gestured contemptuously." riff raff!"

But her father's arrogance knocked the fear out of Sarah and she struck back at him.

"Look I'm over twenty one. I haven't done anything wrong and I don't need you to bail me out thank you!"

"Oh yes you do young lady. You've bitten off a bit more than you can chew and landed us all in the shit!"

She was quite taken aback at this as she had never heard her father swear like that before.

He continued, "You have not told us the complete truth Sarah about your dealings with Martin! The drugs my dear! Any comments?"

Lisa intervened, "No, no -It's not Sarah.... I'm the one... I'm Sorry Sarah I didn't tell you...... I did know why Martin was going down to Gibraltar. There was no job at the Language school in Estepona -that was just to get you to come down here and keep me company. I was working for your Uncle Marcus...."

"How could you not tell me -I thought we knew each other."

"Do you remember that Christmas that Uncle Marcus was down at Penchester Place and he got theatre tickets for us but you couldn't go. That's how we got to know each other. We were lovers too- Can you believe that?" She smiled as she smoked.

"Nothing surprises me at all about you. I'm sorry my daughter ever got mixed up with the likes of you. You're totally amoral. You bewitched my brother -just as you've bewitched my daughter!" Lord Penchester was fuming.

It took several months to sort everything out and Sarah had to return twice to Spain as a material witness in the court cases that were to follow, but her postgraduate studies at St Anselm's Oxford went ahead as planned.

It was a grim foggy November afternoon when she returned to her rooms to find a letter from Piers informing her of all that had transpired since they last met at a court hearing in Malaga. Brenda had been taken seriously ill before the second court hearing and her trial had been postponed. Alas Kurt had died suddenly of a coronary occlusion after attending the final court hearing when his relationship with Guillaume had been exposed and his character impugned by one of the accused. Lisa had been gaoled for her part in Marcus's drugs racket. Piers would be in England for Christmas and wondered if they could possibly get together. They very possibly could.

Sarah still felt pain in her heart at how she had been deceived by Uncle Marcus, Lisa, Kurt and Martin too and how reckless she had been in her sexual indulgence but she felt she had grown up through the experiences or at the least been just plain lucky. Her father had been pompously right at the time but he didn't make a big thing about it afterwards and had been wonderfully supportive since. She was beginning to learn about whom to trust and to learn how diabolically treacherous life can be for the naive and inexperienced. She was startled by the sound of scratching at the door. She went to investigate and found Thomas the college cat which instantly entwined its glistening black body round Sarah's calves. It was a sensual metaphor for what was to follow for who should be climbing the stairs to his rooms opposite but Samson Mensani, a Nigerian student researching Sociology, a 'fresher' like herself whom she was just beginning to know.

"Fancy a coffee Sam?"

He did. Sarah felt a sense of security and purpose in her life and mistakenly thought that this was maturity. She was excited at the prospect of practising her newly felt powers freely on whomsoever she chose. This was the magic spell of her life. The vistas of such a life stretched out ahead of her. It would be a very long time indeed before she fulfilled her destiny, like Brenda before her, within the enclave of San Pedro Del Inglesi.

CPSIA information can be obtained
at www.ICGtesting.com
Printed in the USA
BVHW071133240521
607998BV00004B/531

9 781954 908710